Total-E-1

Relentless
Reckless
Rendered

**Southern Spirits**
A Subtle Breeze
When the Dead Speak
All of the Voices
Wait Until Dawn
Aftermath
What Remains

**Love in Xxchange**
Rory's Last Chance
Miles to Go
Bend
What Matters Most
Ex's and O's
A Bit of Me
A Bit of You

# Leopard's Spots

## LEVI

### BAILEY BRADFORD

Levi
ISBN # 978-0-85715-984-7
©Copyright Bailey Bradford 2012
Cover Art by Posh Gosh ©Copyright February 2012
Interior text design by Claire Siemaszkiewicz
Total-E-Bound Publishing

This is a work of fiction. All characters, places and events are from the author's imagination and should not be confused with fact. Any resemblance to persons, living or dead, events or places is purely coincidental.

All rights reserved. No part of this publication may be reproduced in any material form, whether by printing, photocopying, scanning or otherwise without the written permission of the publisher, Total-E-Bound Publishing.

Applications should be addressed in the first instance, in writing, to Total-E-Bound Publishing. Unauthorised or restricted acts in relation to this publication may result in civil proceedings and/or criminal prosecution.

The author and illustrator have asserted their respective rights under the Copyright Designs and Patents Acts 1988 (as amended) to be identified as the author of this book and illustrator of the artwork.

Published in 2010 by Total-E-Bound Publishing, Think Tank, Ruston Way, Lincoln, LN6 7FL, United Kingdom.

No part of this book may be reproduced, scanned, or distributed in any printed or electronic form without permission. Please do not participate in or encourage piracy of copyrighted materials in violation of the authors' rights. Purchase only authorised copies.

Total-E-Bound Publishing is an imprint of Total-E-Ntwined Limited.

If you purchased this book without a cover you should be aware that this book is stolen property. It was reported as "unsold and destroyed" to the publisher and neither the author nor the publisher has received any payment for this "stripped book".

# LEVI

# Dedication

Because you asked.

# Chapter One

Levi Travis waved goodbye to his sister Jenny and her husband Mark. It'd been good to see them as well as the rest of his large extended family. Once a year there was a reunion held on the Travis ranch. It wasn't really a ranch, though, that's just what everyone called it. They had some horses, but the land itself was mostly raw and unblemished.

The thousand-acre spread, nestled between the mountains in Northwest Colorado, was about the only place a group the size of Levi's family could get together. It wasn't like they could have a beach party. The thick forest, full of Aspens, pines and firs was the perfect place for the snow leopard shifters to run and hunt, although summer was a bit warm. It was better than having the reunion in winter, when tempers could be very touchy. Like snow leopards mated from January through March, so too did the shifter versions of the feline, although they weren't bound to their hormones. They were just…hornier, and the females were more demanding and the males more possessive.

The result was a bunch of grouchy, snarly people and when they shifted? Well, Levi had never seen it, but he'd heard Grandma Marybeth talk about the one time the family had got together in February years back. Apparently there'd been a lot of feline sexing going on, which was something Levi never, ever wanted to think about in regards to his family. It was just best to avoid any potential early mating cycles when the group all got together.

"I am *so* glad the reunion's over with," his brother Oscar muttered. Levi glanced at him, not surprised when he saw Oscar scowling. Oscar tended to scowl a lot. "Please. It's good to see everyone, all sixty-two of them or however many there are now, but geez, it's also good to see them all leave."

Levi snorted even though he did agree with Oscar somewhat. "You know you had fun wrestling with the cousins."

Oscar shook his head. "Yeah, right. I'm just a wild and crazy wrestling fanatic." He held up his right hand, wiggling the two fingers he'd caught in a trap years ago. The middle one had been cut off at the top joint, and the other nearly had, too. "And these are my secret weapons. Makes my foes scream in horror every time I threaten to poke them."

"Cut it out, Oz," Levi scolded, glaring at his younger brother. It wasn't like his fingers were atrociously mangled. In fact, the difference in his finger lengths was hardly noticeable in Levi's opinion. Besides, he seriously doubted many people looked at Oscar's hand once they actually saw him. Oscar was stunningly attractive in an androgynous way Levi had rarely seen and always envied.

With blond hair and pale blue eyes, Oscar was delicate and fair, whereas Levi was tall and bulky, his

## Levi

hair a dark auburn mess and his eyes a muted greenish-grey. Oscar was—there was no other way Levi could think to describe it—beautiful. Maybe years ago, right after the trap accident, there'd been a few rough years when even Levi and the rest of the family had to force themselves not to look at Oscar's fingers, but that was because they all remembered the blood and screams, the snap of the trap as it took off Oscar's fingertips.

But they all got over it. Even Oscar, he'd thought, but maybe not. There been a period of time when Oscar had been younger, and the occasional kid at school had been a jerk but as far as Levi knew, that'd stopped when Oscar ignored it. Hadn't it? Levi had to wonder, because Oscar sure didn't seem as over the trap incident as Levi had believed him to be.

"You make yourself sound like some kind of monster and you're not—as long as you get your caffeine," Levi teased, although an un-caffeinated Oscar was not pleasant to be around. Then again, Levi wasn't all that brilliant or friendly without a cup of coffee or two himself every morning.

Oscar huffed as if he didn't believe a word Levi said, but the pink flush spreading over Oscar's cheeks told Levi his brother had at least heard him.

Levi glanced back in the direction of their cabins. "Do you want help cleaning your place up?" Besides the main house, a sprawling ranch-style that had five bedrooms, there were five smaller cabins scattered over the property, one for each of the siblings.

Well, Jenny's was vacant now since she'd gotten married, although there'd been talk of adding onto hers should she and Mark decide to move back. As usual, though, during the week of the family reunion, they all shared their cabins with whichever family members wanted to crash at the cabins. There'd been several of his male cousins camped out on Levi's floor. It had been fun but exhausting—and messy. He might just need a backhoe to clean his place up.

"Nope. I didn't have very many people staying at my place . Some of the younger kids." Oscar smiled then, looking happier than Levi had seen him in a while. "I bet they didn't make near the mess the guys made at your cabin."

"No shit," Levi grumbled. "I think there's enough beer cans to start my own recycling centre. And don't even get me started on the bathroom." He shuddered, not entirely faking it. His bathroom was a damn nightmare, it was so dirty. Some of his cousins were slobs to the extreme. Next year they could sleep outside, because they sure weren't housebroken, at least not to Levi's standards.

Oscar raised an eyebrow.

Levi could see what he was thinking and moved to head it off before Oscar could offer. "Nope, my fault for not making the morons clean up after themselves. I'll handle it after I have a run."

"Do you want some company?" Oscar asked. "I was going to go read for a while, but if you want, I could come."

"Nah, its fine. After all the togetherness this past week, I could probably use a little time alone." Despite the fact that snow leopards—the non-shifting kind— were solitary creatures, Levi's family was close, often going out together to hunt or just to run. There was another reason Levi declined, too. "Besides, I know you don't particularly enjoy shifting."

Oscar made a rude noise, not quite a word but if it had been, Levi was sure it'd've been worse than the F-word. "It hurts! I know if I did it more, maybe all my ligaments and bones and crap would get used to it or something, but—" Oscar glared at his damaged hand. "Do I *really* need to shift? What's the point in me turning into a snow leopard? I don't have to do it."

Levi silently disagreed. He believed their leopards needed to be released, or...or something would happen, he didn't know what and didn't care to find out. Still, Oscar would shift if Levi nagged enough, which he would do in a day or two. He understood Oscar's aversion to being in his leopard form, considering the steel trap had hurt him when he'd been a curious cub. He just believed Oscar needed to get past the trauma caused from the incident—but not right this instant. "It still hurts when you're used to it, Oz, but it's not unbearable. And it feels really, really good to let go and just run, let the leopard have my mind, sort of."

"You do that, then," Oscar said. He didn't say anything else, just stood beside Levi as the sun began setting. Levi felt strangely edgy, unsatisfied as if his skin itched from head to toe. It was a weird sensation and one he'd not encountered before. The Aspens and pines called to him, promising relief in their shade, in the soil beneath his paws.

Levi shook off his melancholy thoughts and grinned at Oscar. "I'm in a weird mood anyway. Would you let everyone know I'm going out?"

"Sure." Oscar eyed him for a few more seconds. "Be safe." He turned and loped up the pebble path to the house.

Levi sighed and rubbed the back of his neck, observing the pink and orange colours fading in the sky as the sun began to sink further behind a mountain in the distance.

If he was honest with himself, he thought he might be feeling a little envious of some of his cousins. He'd listened as they talked about boyfriends and girlfriends, even casual fuck buddies, but it was the ones who had somebody special, or somebody potentially special, that Levi was jealous of. A petty emotion he wasn't proud of, but he wanted such happiness for himself.

*Maybe if I got out more, went to the bigger cities...* Holton was the nearest town, and calling it a town was charitable. There was a solitary blinking yellow light and a diner that looked decrepit but served the best Mexican food ever. A couple of gas stations, the bare makings of a town, really, and not much more. There wasn't even a school. The few kids in Holton were either bussed or driven to the next closest town, Blankenship, where they joined other kids gathered from tiny towns in the county. Still, it wasn't bad. The people of Holton were generally good-hearted and friendly. It was just lonely for a gay man in this area.

*I need to stop this fricking pity party right now.* Levi crossed over to a pouch tied to a pine. He stripped then stuffed his clothes in the bag before dropping to his knees. The sun began its final farewell for the day, and Levi pressed his palms to the cooling earth, giving himself up to the change. Shifting wasn't instantaneous or painless, but the freedom he had in his feline form was worth any price.

His groan morphed into a mewl as bones popped and muscles rearranged themselves. His jaw ached, his entire skull throbbed then the pain vanished like a bubble bursting. Euphoria replaced the agony and Levi chuffled, the comforting sound tickling his nose when he exhaled. He arched his back and twitched his tail, then growled playfully and bounded off into the woods.

He easily picked out the trail he wanted to take despite the darkness made even more so by the heavy foliage. In minutes he was deep in the forest following a promising scent for dinner. The rabbit was fast, but not fast enough, and Levi pounced, making the kill quick and painless as possible.

Once his stomach was full and his paws licked clean, he lolled on the ground for a while, soaking in the peace he always found here. If he wasn't quite as at peace as usual, he was still okay. Levi knew he wasn't an asshole. He was happy for his cousins, and maybe, if he was lucky, he'd find his own special man. Of course, the man would have to be *really* special—special enough not to look at Levi and judge him by his appearance as so many others did.

Levi was big at six-one and a little over two hundred pounds, and he had rough-hewn features. He'd been told a couple of times his height and build along with his looks made him appear more masculine than the average guy. Looks and all the rest were deceptive, though. None of it meant he was some big dumb brute who wanted to shove down smaller men and fuck them until they screamed.

On the contrary, Levi kind of wanted to be the shoved guy, wanted a little tussle and battle before having another man's strength hold him down. It wasn't that he wanted violence, not force or rape or anything like that. It was a muddle in his mind at times, but what he wanted was someone strong enough to overpower him, but gentle enough not to do so if Levi didn't want to be overpowered. He thought he'd like it, but considering he'd always topped except for one disastrous attempt at bottoming years ago, Levi suspected his fantasy would be better remaining just a fantasy.

Still, even in his leopard form, the thought of being taken was arousing. He imagined a strong body on top of his, a thick cock rutting into him, his faceless, nameless mystery man holding him and shoving Levi against the ground every time he thrust. Levi mewled and clenched the muscles around the pulsing centre beneath his tail. God, but he was randy tonight! If he didn't know better, he'd think he was in heat, something that definitely didn't happen to the males of their species. They were receptive to their females, if they were straight, of course, but—well, he didn't know what was wrong with him tonight. He was off-kilter.

Of course, it probably had a lot more to do with his right hand being his best buddy for the past year. Levi chuffled and rolled onto his belly. He contemplated shifting again just to beat off and relieve the pressure in his balls, but he was enjoying his leopard. And besides, anticipation was at times a very good thing. It might even make his climax, when he finally did beat off, one of those rare, brain-meltingly explosive ones. Once he'd decided to abstain from pleasure for a while longer, he let the streams of moonlight filtering through the leafy branches bathe him and lull him into a light doze. It was contrary to his nature, at least as a snow leopard, but the night breeze was cool, and he was relaxed, so Levi went with it, wrapping his tail around his body and tucking his head between his paws.

# Chapter Two

After weeks of making his way down from Pennsylvania, Lyndon Hines was ready for an unencumbered run. He'd skirted the small town of Holton, Colorado, and come to the brink of a forest he thought was probably part of a state park. If not, someone was sure lucky, because the land was beautiful. There'd been a pull to his gut when he'd looked out the window at the lush foliage, a weird longing vibe had roared up inside him, and Lyndon had needed out immediately. The trucker who'd given him a ride had let him off on the side of the road when Lyndon had asked. Now he was itching to shift and let his cat out.

For the first time in months, he didn't feel hunted — not yet anyway. Something about this area felt right, at least for now. If he wanted to believe it felt a little *more* right than some of the other places he'd encountered in his aimless wanderings, well, there was no harm in hoping. Lyndon felt like he'd been trying to find a place where he belonged all his life. To think he'd never find it would bring him to the brink of a hopelessness he couldn't contemplate. Not if he wanted to survive. Most days he did, or his cougar did.

Sometimes Lyndon wondered what the whole point in going on was. Then he'd get mad at himself for being such a whiny idiot. He hated those moments of doubt when he felt so lost and alone. There was no room for such thoughts in his life. They undermined his confidence, and Lyndon knew it. He tried his best to shake them off and think about what he wanted in life.

Peace. Love. Acceptance. Those were what Lyndon wanted, what he thought he needed. And they had to exist, otherwise he couldn't fathom what the whole point of life was. So Lyndon would stick out his thumb and carry what few belongings he had in the hopes of finding a special place, special people, or just one very unique person who would love him.

This had been his pattern since he'd left Texas. First he'd fled south Texas, chased off by his father who didn't care enough about the human side of them to share his territory. Lyndon wondered how many other siblings he might have roaming about, searching for a home of their own. Maybe they'd come through better adjusted, though. After all, Lyndon could still be doing something with his life, found a different job in marketing or a convenience store, even, and tried harder to live like a normal human being.

He just hadn't fitted into that mould. He'd tried, for years he'd tried, but Lyndon had finally walked in to his apartment one day and didn't just look at it, but *really* saw it for the first time. There was nothing about it that made it feel like home. The walls were white, bare, the furniture sparse and mis-matched in an unattractive manner. But it was more than the look of the place; that, he could have fixed. It was the sheer alienation he felt at that moment, as if he was living someone else's life and it was three sizes too small.

That hadn't been the push that had sent him running, though. No, that impetus had come shortly thereafter when he'd got off work, tired from a particularly rotten day with unhappy clients and unhappier bosses. All he'd wanted to do was collapse into his bed, but was stopped by the pungent odour in his apartment. Virtually everything he'd owned reeked of another cougar marking his territory. Lyndon had been freaked, not recognising the scent of the warning left behind. He knew what it was, but not who had left it. It hadn't been his father who had made him run this last time. His attempt to make a home for himself had already been a failure, but the invasion compounded with it and made staying an unbearable thing for Lyndon to do.

Lyndon had quit his job at the advertising firm he'd worked for in Dallas, not bothering to give notice once his boss snarkily told him it wasn't necessary. Then he'd set about selling everything he couldn't take with him in a duffle, which was most of what he owned. The pervasive feeling of being watched had been disturbing, and Lyndon had got the feeling his time was running out.

He hadn't cared enough to stay and fight — fight who, and for what? So instead Lyndon had left. Ever since then, he'd been searching for — he didn't *know* what, but hoping he'd recognise it when he found it, and trying to escape the sensation of being scrutinised.

That warm, tingling sensation tickling his spine made him think that maybe, this time, he had escaped as he looked at the magnificent trees. After glancing around to make sure no one was around to notice him,

Lyndon cleared a fence then dashed into the dense foliage. He stood there for several minutes, observing, scenting, listening.

Once he was assured it was safe, Lyndon stripped down and tucked his clothes and pack into a cluster of branches. He then spread out on the rough, cool ground and rolled, saturating himself in the smell of the land. Eventually he shifted and saw the forest through sharper eyes, smelt it through a more sensitive nose. His ears twitched at the sounds of prey skittering in the distance.

Lyndon growled softly, the vibrations from the noise rushing down his chest. He flicked his tail as he considered which prey to hunt. He needed a challenge despite the ache in his belly. Tipping his head, he drew the scents deeply into his lungs. *Deer*, his cat yowled, and Lyndon had to agree. As a cougar, he followed the animal's urges to a degree, and a deer would provide a feast for now and more meals for later—if nothing else dug up the remains once Lyndon buried them. That was the cougar's way, and Lyndon had accepted that part of himself the day he'd left Dallas. He'd had to in order to survive. There was no room for a queasy stomach in his current lifestyle.

The trail the deer left behind was tricky, and Lyndon seriously considered going after a rabbit instead, or any available meal. It had been two days since he'd eaten anything more substantial than an energy bar, and his belly was letting him know how displeased it was about that.

Lyndon finally spotted the deer, a lovely doe. She had a healthy build, and Lyndon was contemplating his fine dinner when the doe's head jerked up and she gave a frightened sound. She bolted, running off in a panic. Lyndon started to follow until it occurred to him something had scared the deer, and it hadn't been him. He'd been silent as death stalking his prey, and had been careful to remain downwind. What had spooked the stuffing out of his dinner? The answer came on the breeze, a pungent scent of cat, different from his own. *Not a cougar then, but what the hell else would be out here?* Lyndon racked his brain until a subtle variation in the odour became detectable. Man and beast, combined, and the smell went straight to Lyndon's groin so rapidly it stole his breath. Lyndon huffed and sat back on his haunches, stunned by this new occurrence. He'd figured there were other shifters—why would cougars be the only kind? But he'd never encountered another before.

It wasn't like there was a secret shifter meeting ground or whatever. Well, maybe there was, and he didn't know about it because...it was a secret and all. There'd probably be a secret handshake required to get in, too—and he was mentally babbling, something he tended to do every now and then when his nerves threatened to riot. Curiosity and fear warred against desire, and his cougar's territorial nature was throbbing against his skull, urging him to attack the intruder.

Luckily, Lyndon wasn't just a cougar. He could rationalise and soothe that part of him that sometimes wasn't reasonable. Another deep inhalation calmed his beast more effectively than he could have, though. That tantalising odour sank into him, coiled around his insides and drew him forward on stealthy paws.

Lyndon wasn't exactly calm, however. He was boiling with a need he'd not felt before, and his penis was so hard it ached as it protruded out of its sheath. Lyndon could smell his arousal, was both amused and shocked by it, but more than either of those, he was eager to find the male shifter who caused such a reaction.

The deeper he got into the woods, the stronger and more numerous the scents of other cat shifters became. *There must be a pack or something like it, a feline one here — and I'm likely in their territory.* It would probably have been best to turn and vacate the forest, but Lyndon couldn't, not when there was that one specific, fresher scent of man and cat tugging at his gut. It was like trying to resist chasing a ball of yarn — he just couldn't do it, not when he was in his feline form.

Moonlight dappled the forest floor in patches, casting a silver-white gleam on the ground. The land fell silent around him as creatures held their breath waiting for him to pass. The scent grew stronger and Lyndon slowed his approach even though his body screamed for him to hurry. Eventually he heard a soft chuffling sound from the other feline. He dropped to his belly and crawled forward until he peeked through a clump of fragrant bushes.

What he saw stole his breath and made his joints feel weak and pliable even as his cock and balls throbbed. In a small circular clearing, rolling on the ground on his back, his great big paws up in the air and his plump tail striking up dust and sticks and leaves, was the most beautiful cat Lyndon had ever seen.

The shifter's thick greyish coat was covered in black rosettes, marking him as a leopard. The fur on his belly was longer, paler and looked so soft Lyndon wanted to touch it. Hell, he wanted to rub against the entire cat! Almost as much as he wanted to rub against the man. Lyndon kept still, barely moving at all as he watched the leopard revel in the night.

It wasn't until the other shifter flopped onto his belly and arched his lower back, pushing up his bottom and thrashing his tail from side to side, that Lyndon made a sound. He couldn't help it, need was gnawing at him like a physical ache, making him burns.

It was only a soft sound, a non-threatening rumble that Lyndon couldn't hold back, but the leopard yowled and jumped, spinning and backing up at the same time. Eyes so pale a green they were nearly grey widened when they found Lyndon hiding in the bushes. Lyndon was stunned by the shifter's eye colour. For some reason he'd thought the cat would have the same golden-coloured eyes as his own.

The leopard froze, head down, not blinking as he watched Lyndon. For all that cougars were territorial and aggressive, his cat wasn't feeling either of those things. The urge to mate was on him, overwhelming the other instincts the cougar usually felt. Lyndon had never experienced anything like this, never felt that he had to have someone or else explode from the intensity of the need. He didn't understand it and wondered if it was something he'd have felt for any shifter, or if the magnificent leopard in front of him was special.

Lyndon damned his lack of knowledge about even his own kind of shifters. He wished he knew what to do—listen to that driving instinct to mate, or listen to the human in him who was telling him to use the utmost caution here.

Then the leopard did the one thing that Lyndon couldn't resist, not in his cougar form and probably, he thought, not in his human form either. That gorgeous spotted cat narrowed his eyes and growled low and deep. Not a threat, exactly. To Lyndon's cougar it sounded like a promise of a reward, and as the leopard whirled around and ran, shooting Lyndon a smouldering glance once it was on the move—that was all the encouragement Lyndon needed, especially when the scent of the shifter's arousal was so strong Lyndon was saturated in it. His growl much rougher and full of a vow in return to the leopard's, Lyndon shot out from the bushes to catch his prey.

# Chapter Three

It wasn't fear that propelled Levi away from the cougar, but the potential for his fantasy coming to life. Levi's head was swirling. There were so many thoughts, not the first of which was the fact there were other breeds of shifters. He wondered at his body's instantaneous reaction to the other male, the way an inferno erupted inside him. Levi had never found himself stimulated in this form, not sexually anyway. It was kind of weird and hot at the same time.

And he was throbbing, *oh my God,* his cock and ass and every nerve ending in his body pulsed, amplifying the force of his need. It threatened to consume him and bring him to the sum total of his base needs, all animal and instinct and clawing, biting, a violent mating.

Levi angled to the west, breaking through the foliage and creating a new path. He wasn't completely lost to his lust and didn't want to lead someone who was possibly a threat closer to his family. He didn't know how this would play out, but he could smell the arousal of an unfamiliar male as surely as he could scent his own, so he was fairly certain the trespasser wasn't planning on killing him. *And hopefully, we'll shift...*

The thought alone caused Levi a misstep, and the cougar grew nearer, so much so that Levi felt his hot, moist breath ruffle over his fur. A stinging nip to his tail sent Levi into high gear even as it made his dick weep with his anticipation. The zing of pain from that bite shot up his spine to the tip of his nose in record time and Levi snarled as he whipped his tail.

The cougar's answering swipe of claws, his deep rumbling growl, was all the warning Levi got before a heavy weight slammed into him, onto him. Sharp teeth pierced his nape, enough to sting but not rend, and Levi went down, hard, pinned beneath the cougar.

The rumbling sound his attacker made shot through Levi, starting at his neck and sending his heart into overdrive. He mewled his acquiescence, overcome by scent and touch, the cougar's breath wafting around his head and filling his lungs. A shudder racked the form on top of him, then the body shifted, becoming longer, harder, as an insistent bulge jabbed at his back.

"Shift," the man growled in a voice as rough as his cat's. He gripped Levi's head, burying fingers in his fur and tightening his fist. "Now!"

Levi was astounded and intimidated by the speed of the stranger's transformation. He hesitated and considered throwing him and running, but the possibility of having an experience he'd so desired was an irresistible lure. Levi's mewl twisted into a pain-filled groan as he heaved and shifted, his body aching as the man lifted his weight slightly, holding himself up on one arm. He never once let go of Levi's hair, and when Levi blinked away the burning in his

## Levi

eyes and tried to turn and look aside, his captor rumbled again and bit the same place he'd already marked.

Levi bucked and arched his back; he flailed his arms, looking for something to hold onto. The man dropped onto his back again, knocking the breath from Levi's lungs. A heavy, hard cock prodded his ass and Levi's wrists were grabbed, the left first then the right. Both were then pinned above his head.

He could have broken free of the hold, Levi didn't doubt it, but everything about this felt surreal and too perfect to risk bringing to a halt. He clenched his hands in the hold, though, and was rewarded with a tighter grip and a harder bite, and the alarming jab of a cockhead against his hole.

"You want me to let you go?" Levi was asked as his pucker was rubbed again.

Levi tried to shake his head, but the grasp on his wrists was implacable. "No," he rasped, his throat nearly as tight as the hold the man had on him. "Please—" Levi might just cry if he ended up left there, unfulfilled. Levi's dick had never been so hard in his life, and his skin felt super-sensitised, every twig and grain of dirt, every place his body was touching the cougar's sizzled and twitched as need that tied him in knots inside. "Please," he said again, closing his eyes as he rolled his hips what little he could. "I need—*something!*" *Anything, just have tc come!*

The raspy laughter reminded Levi of the chuffling sound snow leopards made, and it eased some of the tension threatening to shatter him into a billion pieces. He hissed softly as his hair was released, the sudden lack of pressure making his scalp sting and tingle in an almost maddening way.

Before Levi could catch more than a glimpse of white teeth and golden hair, the man on top of him pressed his cheek to Levi's. Their breath mingled as Levi's ass was spread. Hot and heavy, his cock slid into Levi's crease, shooting sparks of need up from Levi's ass.

"Damn it," was muttered in his ear, then Levi couldn't hear anything other than his pulse and their grunts, and the sound of skin slapping skin.

Levi's cock was wedged uncomfortably between him and the ground, but somehow the cougar shifter managed to shove his hand under Levi and grip his aching length. Every thrust between his ass cheeks rocked Levi's hips into the ground and his cock into the hand fisting his shaft.

Levi whined and keened, cursed and begged as his hole clenched, eager to be filled, but the stranger didn't press in, keeping his rutting to short, hard thrusts that burned along Levi's crack.

"In me," Levi demanded, but the man wouldn't be swayed, only groaning and biting Levi's jaw in response. Levi wanted to shout in frustration—he wanted it all, even though he knew, he *knew* better than to fuck without condoms and some kind of lube. Spit would do in a pinch, but it'd leave him hurting pretty badly. Yet knowing that didn't make him want to be fucked any less.

Then the man squeezed Levi's cockhead hard enough to make him see stars, and delved a nail into his slit. Levi forgot about his needy ass and screamed when spunk poured from his dick. He shook from all the way to his toes and his head jerked back as if pulled on a string. The shifter rolled off him and flipped Levi over while Levi gasped and his vision blurred. A warm, heavy weight settled on his waist and Levi blinked away his fuzzy vision in time to see moonlight caressing cut muscles and golden hair. Eyes the same shade as that hair flashed at him, then a shout splintered the air and cum hit Levi's jaw.

Levi knew he had to be gaping like an idiot, but he was shocked. He hadn't expected to be marked like that, covered in another man's scent. It seemed possessive and feral and he was reading too much into it, he knew he was! He tried to get such ridiculous thoughts out of his head as he watched for the next spurt from the thick cock the man was stripping with hard, rough strokes. Abs rippled with each jet of spunk sprayed. The fourth bit splattered onto Levi's stomach, and all he could scent, all he could see, was the man on top of him, now purring as he slowly rubbed his dick.

Then he stopped, and Levi tensed, knowing his fantasy was coming to an end. Those golden eyes narrowed at him while Levi absorbed every detail of his temporary lover's face. He was sharp-angled cheeks and stubborn firm jaw, flashing eyes and thin lips, and he was the sexiest man Levi had ever seen. Bigger than him, stronger, probably. And fixing to be gone.

"Is this your land?" he asked Levi.

Levi was hesitant to answer, but lying would get him nowhere. Surely the cougar could scent a lie just as Levi usually could. "Yes," he answered, then blurted out, "and my name is Levi, in case you give a damn about introductions." He was unsurprised when he quickly found himself alone on the ground before he even finished speaking. Levi knew he'd just broken some unwritten one-off rule.

"I liked our introduction just fine the way it was, but one thing—cougars aren't known for sharing, Levi."

the man said, then faster than Levi had thought possible, he shifted and was gone.

Levi was left alone to try to figure out what his mysterious man had meant and what the hell had just happened besides the obvious.

# Chapter Four

*What. The. Hell!* Lyndon ran, forgetting about his need for food. Right now, he needed to figure out why he'd all but attacked the lovely leopard shifter. *Levi. God, even his name is sexy!* As lovely as the cat had been, the man was even more so. Rough, broad jaw and strong, firm muscles, there'd been nothing weak or small about him. His cock in Lyndon's hand had felt huge, and when Lyndon had flipped Levi over, even as it softened Levi's penis been an impressive sight.

And to have been given Levi's strength! Lyndon had no illusions about that. While he may have been bigger and a little more muscular than Levi, they were likely equally matched. If the Levi had wanted to, he could have thrown Lyndon off and tried to beat the shit out of him. Maybe even succeeded, considering the way Lyndon was so attracted to him. But Levi hadn't done either of those things, instead going still and compliant beneath Lyndon and even begging Lyndon to fuck him.

Lyndon had wanted to, God had he wanted to! But two things had seeped into his lust-filled brain, helping him find the restraint he'd been searching for so desperately. The first had been the minutes it had taken Levi to shift. Lyndon had thought perhaps he'd bitten too hard when he'd brought the leopard down, even though he hadn't sunk his teeth into muscle, just skin. As soon as the transformation was complete, however, his senses had told him the only thing wrong with the man was that he was so aroused he ached from it.

Second, though, was the lack of sufficient supplies — lube and condom — added to Lyndon's own need, which was too great for finesse or the time it would have taken to prepare the man's ass for penetration. It had required every bit of Lyndon's self-control to keep from thrusting his dick in Levi's hole and fucking him into unconsciousness — which likely would have come quickly due to the pain such an entry would have caused.

So Lyndon had taken what was offered, just not completely, not like he'd really wanted to do. Still, feeling those firm cheeks squeezing his length had nearly melted his brain. It had only been instinct and a desire to hear and smell Levi come that had given Lyndon enough sense to palm his dick.

And Levi had been beautiful in his release, the sounds he had made, the way his body tensed, muscles rippling as his spine lengthened and stretched. Never had Lyndon experienced such a sexual encounter so intensely, so thoroughly. How would he keep himself from hunting Levi down again? Why should he bother to restrain himself?

He didn't know if he could.

Lyndon reached his clothes and bag, his mind remaining on Levi. His stomach rumbled, reminding him he'd neglected it for too long. Instead of turning back and tracking down dinner, he shifted and dressed, keeping an ear out for any approaching animal. He sort of hoped Levi would follow him and couldn't quite bury his disappointment when he made it out of the tree line without so much as that tingly feeling one had when being watched.

Well, it was his own fault. He could have stayed and talked to Levi. Why hadn't he? What had he been thinking, to spew some bullshit line about cougars not sharing? They didn't, though, not their territories at least. However, Lyndon wasn't sure that was what he'd meant. Somehow, in that brief and electric encounter, he'd made Levi his in his mind. Stupid, considering. What did Lyndon have to offer? Months of bumming around the country while he whined to himself that he didn't belong anywhere and ran from a twisted stalked her couldn't identify.

What an ass he'd been. What a scared child, running, always running—just like he had when his father, Cole Tavares, had come after him. When he really thought about it, Lyndon knew he wasn't much of a man at all no matter how masculine he looked. A man would stand his ground. Lyndon hadn't yet, and he'd started this pattern of fleeing when he'd met his father for the first time.

Lyndon had let his human feelings overtake his cougar nature in regards to his father. It had hurt, having his father drive him away. Lyndon still didn't understand why the man was like he was, disdainful of their human nature even though he was a successful man in the human world. He wanted the wealth and glory that entailed, but none of the emotions a human had. Instead he treated Lyndon like an invader in his life. Lyndon had been raised by his mother, a human who'd not known what his father was, at least not at first. It wasn't until after Cole had impregnated her that she'd known the child she was carrying wasn't exactly human. Then the bastard had dropped some money in a bank account and left. Lyndon's mother had told him the story repeatedly, and while his mom hadn't always been stable, she'd never been a liar.

It wasn't until after her death that his old man had even deigned to make an appearance and introduce himself, and even then it was only so he could threaten Lyndon and force him out of his home in San Antonio. Lyndon had had little choice but to accept the money his father had given him, along with the truth about what they were—cold hearted beasts destined to be alone. To prove his point, his father had shifted and attacked. Lyndon had learned to shift quickly by then but he'd never even encountered another cougar shifter or any shifter for that matter, and he hadn't had a clue how to fight. He had the scars from the one and only encounter with his father to this day.

If he hadn't actually found another cougar shifter— one a hell of a lot more human in nature than his father—Lyndon would probably be dead. Grady Marks had taken Lyndon in after finding him torn up and hurting, dumped in a scrub-filled area to the south of San Antonio. He'd been kind, a good man and shifter, and he'd taught Lyndon a few things about what he was. Grady hadn't known a lot about what they were himself, professing to be a loner and liking it that way. Yet he'd been nothing but patient with Lyndon. He'd even made sure Lyndon did something, made something of himself at least for a while. Grady had asked Lyndon what he wanted, and it'd been easy to answer at the time. He wanted to be a normal kid, like everyone who wasn't a damn shifter. College had been the obvious choice, and for a while Lyndon was almost happy. Then Grady had died and nothing felt right. Grady had been gone for a while now, and Lyndon knew the man's death was the catalyst that had sent him running, or searching, he wasn't sure which it was anymore. Really, his head was a damned mess, wasn't it? What rational man would have walked away from a well-paying job even if he had hated it? Especially in today's fucked up economy.

Lyndon shrugged. At least he still had some money in the bank. He'd used what his father had given him to get his business degree, but he'd always tucked a small part of his cheque into savings. After paying for Grady's funeral, Lyndon's savings had almost been wiped out. Since he thumbed most rides and slept out in the open when he could—which was more often than not, considering what he could shift into—Lyndon hadn't touched much of what money he had left.

But he thought he might tonight. It had been too long since he'd slept in a bed and had a long, hot shower. Bathing in streams could suck, and he'd paid for the occasional shower at the truck stops, but often there simply wasn't time between rides to enjoy a shower. Plus, if it were crowded, it didn't pay to piss off the other men who were waiting, not if he was hoping to bum a ride from one of them. This morning he'd got a lukewarm shower at a stop outside of Jenkins, but after today's exertions—

Lyndon sniffed and closed his eyes as the musky scent of cum reached his nose. He saw Levi again, resignation already showing in those pale eyes, Lyndon's cum splattered on his body. God, but he wished he'd ran his hands over that warm flesh, covered it in his spunk so thoroughly the leopard shifter would never get the scent off. If he'd fucked him, marked him from the inside out—Lyndon snorted.

What the *hell* was wrong with him? It wasn't like he hardly ever got laid. There were, not surprisingly, a large number of horny guys in the world. A lot of them happened to be truckers eager to spread their cheeks for Lyndon. He thought it might have more to do with what he was than how he looked, as if humans could detect the undercurrent of the beast inside him.

It was several miles into Holton. Lyndon walked the distance in the dark and didn't see a single vehicle along the way. It was late, almost midnight by the time he reached the lone hotel in town. The place looked to be well-maintained, which Lyndon hoped meant plenty of warm water. He checked his reflection in the window before he entered and smoothed down his long hair. At least he had on decent jeans and shirt, and had managed to shave that morning, so he didn't look like the vagrant he was.

Inside, the lobby smelt clean, a little like artificial pine cleaner, but that was better than many alternatives. Lyndon stepped over to the counter and saw the sign informing customers to ring the bell if they needed help. A tap of his finger made the thing clang irritatingly, but less than thirty seconds later a perky young woman came out from what might have been an office. Her blue eyes rounded as she swept her gaze over his face and torso. Lyndon wished he'd worn something other than the tight, long-sleeved T-shirt.

"Can I help you?" she all but purred in a way that did absolutely nothing for him.

Regardless, he plastered on a smile that probably looked as fake as it felt and dug his wallet out of his back pocket.

"I need a room. I'm not sure for how long, maybe two or—no, three days? At least." Who knew if he'd stay that long, but maybe he would. It didn't have anything to do with the man he'd met, Lyndon told himself. He was just tired of moving around and wanted some time to rest and not worry about where he was going. The latter *was* true, but Lyndon knew the first part of his reasoning wasn't. Levi intrigued him, and Lyndon felt like he'd been caught in a sensual snare he wasn't certain he wanted to be free of.

"That'll be one-ten." The woman—her name tag proclaimed her to be Dahlia D—rested an elbow on the counter and leant forward.

"That's fine. Cash okay?"

She looked at him for a long moment then nodded. "Usually we require a credit card, but I can make an exception."

Lyndon casually moved a step back to avoid contact with Dahlia D's large breasts and took his licence and most of the cash he had on him and handed it over. As Dahlia D took care of registering him then getting his receipt and key card, Lyndon debated the wisdom of using his ATM card to access the rest of his savings. After assuring Dahlia D that he would let her know if he needed 'anything at all', Lyndon made his way to his room. It was small but clean, the mattress firm and comfortable when he gave it a test sprawl. His stomach growled and cramped, and Lyndon sat up, rubbing his belly. He gave the rest of the room a cursory inspection—beige walls, paisley wallpaper trim, crappy landscape prints that seemed to be a requirement for hotels of this sort, as well as cheap-looking furniture.

The dresser held a decent-size TV and a few drawers for his scant belongings. The matching faux cherry wood nightstand contained two religious books in the drawer and a lamp and alarm clock on the top. A small desk that also served as a table took up one corner and a paisley print chair the other. The carpet was a rather hideous shade of blue, but clean.

Lyndon walked over and peeked in the bathroom, grunting at the size of the tub. Too small for him, but he preferred showers anyway. He'd need to buy some shampoo and—he leaned in far enough to check his appearance in the bathroom mirror—maybe even conditioner. It'd been a long time since he'd bothered trying to tame his hair. There was no point in trying to lie to himself about his reasons for fretting over it now. If he should happen to run into Levi... Well, he wanted to look his best. There was probably some instinctive thing to it, a subconscious need to appear capable and attractive and all the kinds of stuff people had been doing to attract a mate since time began.

Lyndon didn't want to dwell on such complexities right now. He wasn't particularly capable, and as for attractive, he was just all right. Not model-handsome, but he wasn't a guy who'd look better with a bag over his head, either. And his body was pretty damn tight. Not that he was vain, either, at least not normally.

Now wasn't the time to start either. Lyndon turned away from the mirror. He'd depress himself if he kept checking himself out, all shaggy-haired and worn around the eyes. It seemed to him the traces of his youth were long gone, and maturity was kind of a scary look on him.

Remembering the convenience store he'd spotted on his way to the hotel, Lyndon decided to go and grab what he needed, including some kind of food and drinks. He had about forty bucks on him, he thought. Not a lot, but if he was frugal he could make it last for a few days at least. Using the ATM was something he tried to avoid since he wasn't sure his movements weren't being monitored that way, but it looked like he was going to have to take the chance. Even if he found a job, it'd be a while before he got paid.

*And why the hell am I thinking about getting a job here?* Lyndon hadn't hung around anywhere long enough to get a job, not since he'd left Dallas. Making a mental list of what he would need, he made sure the hotel room door was locked. A short jog across the parking lot and up a block, then he was walking into the brightly lit store. A few old men sat at booths built for two. Lyndon glanced at the clock above the cash register, surprised to find it was after one in the morning. He shrugged internally. Maybe if he lived to be old he'd hang out somewhere like this at night, unless he had someone warm to sleep beside instead.

Memories of Levi, both man and beast, and the odd merging of him being both and neither flitted through Lyndon's mind. He had a feeling he was going to have to get used to thinking about him.

Lyndon winced as he picked up the cheapest conditioner on the shelf. It was a crappy brand and overpriced by at least two bucks, but there was no way the stuff at the hotel was going to be enough. He hated buying necessities from places like this, where everything was so marked up the prices should have been considered robbery. Lyndon stared at the bottle and wondered again what he was doing. Should he go after Levi? But what did he have to offer?

Nothing, really, is what he kept coming back to. But if he stayed here, maybe found work and became a productive member of society again, then he wouldn't be such a bad bet. And this was a small town, so chances were good he'd run into Levi here, sooner rather than later.

Just the idea of seeing Levi again set Lyndon's pulse to fluttering in a way he'd have been embarrassed about if anyone else had known. He tucked the conditioner under his arm and picked out a shampoo and soap. Some hideously expensive toothpaste and a few other things to groom himself with, along with a six pack of sodas and snacks, and Lyndon was looking at a little over thirty bucks in products he could have got cheaper at a real store.

The clerk snapped his gum and held out his hand. "That'll be thirty-two twenty-three."

Lyndon eyed the man, his name tag proclaiming him to be Craig. He looked young, but not much younger than Levi, maybe. But what would Lyndon ask him? And was Levi out here? Lyndon put thirty-three dollars in Craig's hand and almost yelped in surprise when Craig tickled his palm.

Craig winked at him and gave his crotch a lascivious look. Lyndon was torn between feeling flattered and feeling dirty. He settled on grabbing his bag and bolting from the store. Craig could do whatever with his change.

It wasn't until he was back in his room, reluctantly washing away the scent of Levi's cum, that it occurred to Lyndon he might have over-reacted to Craig's come-on. The clerk had been cute in a pixie-ish sort of way, but Lyndon's stomach had fairly turned inside out just from Craig's touch. Weird, considering he'd fucked much less attractive men before, but the truth of his reaction was even stranger, and more than a little scary.

Craig had touched him, and Lyndon's mind and body had rebelled, even his cat had rebelled. He didn't want to be touched by anyone other than Levi. It was the truth, and he wasn't sure what he was going to do about it.

# Chapter Five

Levi spent a good hour or more lying on the ground trying to make sense of what had happened. Eventually, he forced himself to get up and debated shifting again, but he didn't have the energy. Giving in to the urge pushing at him, he followed the cougar shifter's trail, able to pick out broken branches and crushed leaves, the pawed clumps of dirt where the other cat had high-tailed it off the property. His senses weren't quite as sharp as when he was in snow leopard form, but they were good enough that Levi found the place where the man's scent, still somewhat fresh, headed back towards Holton. Levi was tempted to keep following him, but what would be the point? He'd been left behind, after all, and Levi did have his pride.

The trip back to his cabin left Levi a confused mess. Part of him still wanted to chase down the cougar shifter, but another part, the more insistent part, wanted to go home and revel in the memory of what had happened between them even while Levi cursed the man for running away. That was what he'd done, tucked his tail and hauled kitty ass like Levi had turned into a lion or whatever it was that could eat a cougar. And what had he said? Like Levi even had to think about it. *Cougars aren't known for sharing.* Levi snorted as he opened the door to his cabin, forgetting the place was a disaster until he went inside and it wasn't. "What—"

Oscar came out of the bathroom, wearing long rubber gloves and holding a toilet brush. He looked at Levi and wrinkled his nose. "My book was beyond boring. You smell like semen." He sniffed and his eyes bugged as he pointed the wet brush at Levi. "And not *your* semen, not just, anyway! What the heck happened?" He came closer, waving that nasty brush.

Levi stepped back and pressed himself against the door. "Why are you here so late? It has to be after midnight. And could you not splatter me with whatever's dripping off of that? I'd rather not add eau de crapper to my already noxious—to you at least—odour."

Oscar blinked then looked at the toilet brush like he hadn't a clue how it'd ended up in his hand. He scrunched his nose up again and muttered something about 'nasty uncouth heathens' and 'their freakish bowels and sorry aim pissing' as he strode to the bathroom, his usual grace missing. Levi heard a thud of plastic on porcelain and the *phthpt* of the glove being pulled off, then Oscar marched back in, a determined glint in his eye.

"I told you I was bored, that's why I came over here. Sit and spill." Oscar pointed to the couch, which was now recognisable as something other than a pile of empty food wrappers and cans.

Levi braced a hand on the back of the couch and leapt over it, landing on his butt and jostling the springs under the cushions. He craned his neck and grinned at Oscar, who merely rolled his eyes before doing the exact same thing and landing beside Levi, except Oscar moved like grace personified as he did it. Oscar nibbled his bottom lip while he faced Levi expectantly.

Levi sighed and leaned his head back against the top of the couch. The bite at the nape of his neck stung and he hissed. Next thing he knew, Oscar was practically climbing on him, pushing at him plucking at the back of Levi's shirt.

"Holy crap!" Oscar tugged some more until Levi finally gave in and slumped forward. He prodded at the bite, eliciting a grunt from Levi. "Geez, what did you do—or, what *did* you?"

Oscar's eyes were so huge Levi didn't know why they weren't shooting right out of the sockets.

"Oh my God," Oscar gasped, slapping a hand to his chest. "Did you, you know, in leopard form? Did you have sex with a wild cat?"

He couldn't decide whether Oscar was horrified or titillated at the idea and he didn't have the energy to try. The truth was, Levi had come down hard after his fantasy man had run off. *More proof the whole thing really happened, in case I ever doubted. The ending sucked!* Levi gave himself a mental shake and nudged Oscar's arm until his brother sat down beside him without poking or prodding at Levi.

Oscar listened in rapt attention to Levi's recounting of his run, although the sexual encounter was abbreviated to a 'and he rubbed off on me after I came', in an attempt by Levi to mute the strength of the experience in his mind. Besides, that was more than he had ever wanted to share about his sex life while talking to his baby brother.

"What did he look like?"

Levi was stumped by Oscar's question, because there just weren't enough words, not the right ones that Levi could find, at least. He settled for giving what he figured would be a corny answer to Oscar. "He was golden, Oz. Gorgeous, big, and golden, even under the silver moonlight."

"Wow."

*Yeah, that almost covers it.* Levi watched Oscar rolling something around in his mind. He almost dreaded finding out what it was, but knew he had little choice in the matter. Levi always listened to Oscar even if sometimes he didn't like what his brother said. This time it wasn't too bad, though, and was something Levi had been thinking about, too.

"So there are other shifters," Oscar mused. "That makes sense, though. But how much of their animal's nature do they retain?"

Levi was wondering the same thing. "He said cougars aren't big on sharing."

Oscar tapped his lips, muffling his voice lightly when he spoke. "Was he talking about you, I wonder?"

"Right, that's why he took off like a cat whose tail got stomped on." Admitting it was almost as humiliating as the actual occurrence.

"Ouch." Oscar grimaced, moving his hand down to rub at his backside. "Don't remind me. But think about it. We aren't solitary creatures like snow leopards are. We kind of have our own pack, even if it is all family. Are we that way because of what we are, or despite it?"

Sometimes Oscar could tie even himself up with words, but Levi thought he caught the gist of what his brother was saying. "Grandma Marybeth said that unlike the full-blooded snow leopards, she was part of a family of shifters, kind of a village or clan somewhere around the Himalayas. Makes me think we are more human, and we just have something extra, maybe, instead of a wild beast tempered by a little humanity." Levi shrugged.

"I wish we knew more about what we are," Oscar grumbled. "All we know is what Grandma Marybeth tells us."

Levi did, too, but since Grandma Marybeth was the only link they had to their history, and she hadn't been more than a young child when her shifter clan had been hunted and killed for their fur and parts, she didn't know very much about their shifter history either. They did know the ability to shift came from the maternal line, passed from mother to children. Even male shifters couldn't help populate their species. It tended to make him feel superfluous, but the fact was it certainly made being gay easier for his family to accept. Which was good, considering there seemed to be quite a few of his cousins who were also gay. And there was Uncle Victor and his partner Clement—

"Go shower already," Oscar ordered, snapping Levi out of his thoughts. "Don't forget to check your website for new orders before you go to bed, either!"

Levi heaved himself up off the couch, Oscar shoving on his butt to help him out, or more likely, just to irritate him by implying Levi needed help in the first place. If so, it didn't work. Levi wasn't up to being snarky. "Thanks for cleaning up the place. I appreciate it." He reached out and ruffled Oscar's hair, something his little brother only tolerated from him, although usually not for long.

Oscar swatted at Levi's hand and ducked away. "I told you, I was bored. See you in the morning."

Levi stopped at the bathroom door and turned to look at Oscar, who was watching him with an odd expression on his face. "Can you—will you not tell anyone else about this? I don't care to share my sex life with the family. It's just weird." And he wanted to keep the memory of tonight for himself. He hadn't had any choice but to explain to Oscar since he'd been here and Levi had smelt like cum.

Oscar nodded after several seconds but it seemed a reluctant gesture. "I won't say anything—for now. If the cougar shows back up or hurts you, though, I'm going to make sure everyone in this family goes after him."

Levi figured that was all he could really ask for. "Thank you." He winked at Oscar then turned around and entered the bathroom.

Since his bathroom was no longer trashed and the toilet clean enough that the porcelain bowl sparkled, Levi almost felt like he was going to soil the tidy room. Almost, but not entirely. Sure, he was covered in dirt and twigs and probably a few ticks even, but he also carried his mystery shifter's scent and seed.

Stripped, Levi stood in front of the mirror above the sink and twisted around until he could see the bite mark like he'd been itching to do. It wasn't deep, had barely broken the skin in a couple of places, but it was a deep purple-red that reminded Levi of the other man's thick cock as he'd pumped it, emptying his load onto Levi's skin.

Levi's cock sprung back to full staff, heat pooling low in his gut, spearing through his groin and tightening everything from his belly to his calves. He did his best to ignore his arousal until he started the shower running. His cock bobbed against his stomach, leaving sticky spots in the dark hair that was smattered over the front of his torso. He wished he had more willpower, at least enough to wash the cum off him first, but Levi just didn't.

He rested his ass on the countertop and spread his legs, wiggling until his cheeks were parted as well. Levi closed his eyes and ran his hand down his jaw, regretting having already scraped the cum from his skin there. He traced the places where the stranger's creamy essence had all but singed his skin.

Those spots felt warmer, more sensitive, and if that was only his imagination, Levi didn't care. He thought he could come just from brushing over them again and again.

Not that he was going to.

Levi gasped as he fisted his dick in a strangling grasp. The bite of pain pushed him closer to the edge. Reaching behind himself, Levi used his other hand and pulled at his ass. He traced the path rubbed by a thick cock earlier. His skin there was tender, almost raw, and patches of dried, flaky pre-cum gave way under his touch. Levi moaned, softly at first then louder as he jerked his cock without mercy.

Already his balls were tight, high in their sac. His thighs quivered and waves of stinging heat rolled from his groin to his ass, from his belly to his nipples. Each stroke of his cock reverberated to pleasure points he hadn't even known he had, setting his body into a frenzy of chaotic need. Levi let the images come — golden hair, golden eyes, golden skin, the snarl and sound he'd heard as he'd been mounted.

*Fuck, but I wish* — Levi got no further than that before he keened as ecstasy exploded up from his balls, bathing his entire being in a sensation so intense it rivalled the earlier encounter in the forest. Levi pumped his cock, kept stripping it even after the last spit of cum had drained.

It wasn't enough, despite his dick being raw and sore from his rough handling along with being ground against the forest floor a few hours ago. Even though he doubted he'd get hard again for hours, Levi still wasn't sated. He didn't understand it and he sure as hell didn't like it, feeling that he was controlled by something outside of *his* control. The more Levi thought about it, the angrier he got.

*At least that's better than mooning over some freaky-hot dry hump session. I can rail at fate, or whatever. Or, I can act like a man and get my shit together before I become a simpering metrosexual or, God forbid, a sensitive soul.*

That was disturbing enough to knock Levi out of his weird funk. He scrubbed his body clean, refusing to regret the loss of another man's scent, and told himself he wouldn't think of the cougar shifter again.

It wasn't a resolution he could keep, not even for a few minutes after he made it. Levi dreamt of his mysterious lover and woke up so aroused he wanted to scream. Masturbating wasn't cutting it. He craved a touch that wasn't his own, a specific touch from a specific man.

Levi hoped the need would lessen as time passed, but he had a bad feeling it wouldn't. No one had ever got to him so intensely, and he was afraid he'd have a difficult time shaking thoughts of his sexy trespasser. It wouldn't surprise him if he ended up thinking of the golden man every day and continued dreaming of him at night no matter how much he tried to forget.

Levi scoffed at his ridiculous musings. What was he, some hopelessly romantic sap? Was he going to wait around to see if his one true love returned? Sarcastic or not, the idea gave him a warm, quivery feeling in his stomach. It also sent his cock straight into overdrive, bringing it to fully erect in seconds.

Which Levi ignored. He needed to learn some restraint, especially since he had no intention of trying to hunt down someone who couldn't get away from him fast enough. He was damn well going to have to get over his growing obsession, and he would start by keeping himself so busy he didn't have time to dwell on anything other than his work.

# Chapter Six

Almost a full week after the hottest sexual encounter Lyndon had ever had, he'd found himself hanging around Holton. He'd hitched a couple of towns over to withdraw more money from his account, hoping the distance between Holton and Jeffers would throw off whoever had been on his trail for months. But within a few days, a familiar sensation began prickling the fine hairs at his nape.

Off and on he felt hunted, watched, though he couldn't pinpoint where the feeling was coming from or who was causing it. Someone was, that much he knew. Usually he ran when he became aware of being hunted, but this time he decided to stand his ground. He was tired of this game, and eventually he would be caught by whoever it was pursuing him. Holton seemed as good a place as any for that confrontation.

Meanwhile, he needed to eat. He didn't have much money, and what he did have wouldn't hold him for much longer. Lyndon had been looking for work in the small town. So far he hadn't had any luck at all, but he wasn't ready to give up. He had memories of Levi constantly filling his mind.

Lyndon kept hoping to see him, but in the week he'd been in town, he hadn't caught so much as a whiff of Levi. Lyndon had put off going back to the wooded area where he'd met him for several reasons, not the least of which was fear for his own life. He didn't know about all the other scents he'd picked up there while still in cougar form. There were other leopards in those woods, or there had been. Lyndon doubted they'd be as friendly as his snow leopard had been.

And Lyndon kept thinking of Levi as his, which was weird but he couldn't stop it and gave up trying a couple of days ago. He had found out what breed of leopard Levi was, thanks to the small library a few blocks over from his hotel. He wondered what a snow leopard — what several snow leopards — were doing in Colorado, half of the world away from where they originated. There were so many questions Lyndon had, but what he really wanted was to touch Levi again, to smell him and feel that powerful body beneath him.

The intensity of the sensation of being watched ramped up suddenly. It was so strong his spine nearly vibrated with it. He stood in Jambree's, the diner, trying to talk the owner into hiring him to bus tables or cook, whatever he could get. Lyndon was growing desperate, and jobs in a town this size were scarce.

His neck itched and Lyndon just kept from reaching around and scratching it. He began to have second thoughts about staying here, not because he was scared, but because he was bringing danger to this town. Maybe it was only to himself — no one else who'd been around him had been hurt so far, not that he knew of. Why was he worrying about that now, anyway? He doubted Levi wanted to find him.

It'd been stupid to think, to hope. Really, he should have known better, especially after the way he'd treated the guy, leaving him lying on the ground covered in cum. Yeah, Lyndon was a real catch. Levi had probably scrubbed Lyndon's spunk off him and never given Lyndon another thought.

But someone had been thinking of him, he could feel the intensity in the hidden stare that stroked his back. Lyndon nodded at Mr Hernandez as the man went on about the economy sucking. As if Lyndon weren't aware of that. His savings were dwindling rapidly. It didn't help that he'd been buying food rather than hunting, and paying for the hotel room, but he'd remembered the scent of other shifters in those woods and thought after the way he'd done Levi, it might be wiser to stay away from that area unless Lyndon wanted to risk being strung up or shot. But he'd kind of thought if they saw each other in town, as men, they could talk—or Lyndon could grovel.

Lyndon had thanked Mr Hernandez for his time and walked out of the diner, his hands tucked into the pockets of his light jacket to hide the way he'd fisted them. He was tired of feeling hunted, tired of trying to figure out *why* he was being hunted. Knowing how territorial a cougar could be, he could understand it in the wild, but he, and whoever was chasing him, were not simply cougars. They were human beings, too, capable of logic and emotions and reason, although maybe his stalker wasn't. Obviously his stalker wasn't.

Outside, Lyndon looked around as casually as possible. He didn't spot anyone out of place in his first visual sweep, and he'd become somewhat familiar with the town in the past week. Lyndon was observant, had to be to survive, so the fact that he couldn't find who was watching him was a kick to his pride. As much as he'd like to believe he was just being paranoid, he couldn't, not when he'd woken up in a nice wooded area in Pennsylvania only to find scat from another cougar not far from where he'd rested. Just in case he might have possibly missed that sign, the other cougar had clawed as many trees as possible, and left a rotting deer carcass at the exact place Lyndon had entered the area.

The shifter could have attacked him, could have brought this creepy game of cat and mouse to an end. That he hadn't told Lyndon the guy was really a sick bastard who enjoyed the hunt, enjoyed toying with him. Well, *he* wasn't enjoying this one bit, and it would end. Whether that entailed his death or the other shifter's remained to be seen.

Lyndon was so lost in his thoughts he almost didn't notice the cute little blond man getting out of a big black dually pickup. Carelessness like that could cost Lyndon his life. Granted, sometimes he thought he might not care if it did, but those were low moments that usually passed quickly. He'd better get his head on straight and be more alert if he wanted any chance at all with Levi. *Don't even go there. He wouldn't have me, not now.*

Lyndon scooted to the edge of the sidewalk when the blond headed his way. He glanced into the young man's pale blue eyes and was struck to find him not only glaring, but veering right into Lyndon's path— and not looking like he was going to back down or stop. Something eased in his chest, a knot of worry that he'd been found. Whoever this stranger was, Lyndon didn't think he was the same man who'd hunted him. Was this why he'd felt watched? Lyndon thought it must be, with the way those blue eyes never left him. He wondered what he'd done to attract this man's attention.

For whatever reason, he seemed determined to get in Lyndon's way. Lyndon was both curious and irritated enough to let him. *This might be amusing.* Lyndon arched a brow at the guy then veered off into a small alley between the miniscule hardware store and a thrift shop. He'd be surprised if the guy had the balls —

"You're a dick, you know it?"

*All right, he definitely has more balls than sense.* Lyndon figured it was a good thing it was mid-morning, otherwise the lunch crowd — such as it was — would be out and about, and this budding confrontation would be witnessed when he'd rather it not be. Lyndon turned halfway back between the wood-framed buildings and gave him a seething glare. It didn't seem to faze the man — boy? He looked really young — a bit.

The blond stalked up to him and thrust a finger in Lyndon's face. Lyndon couldn't help but notice the missing parts to a couple of his digits. He cringed before he could catch himself and saw his reaction register in the way the other man's expression darkened.

"You're the gold bastard who was on our property a week ago," the younger man snarled.

Lyndon kept very still as the man's scent finally reached him. If he'd been in cougar form, he'd have noticed it a lot sooner. There was a familiar tang to it that Lyndon recognised as belonging to a shifter, a snow leopard if he wasn't mistaken. It wasn't identical to Levi's, wasn't the one that still made Lyndon's dick hard every time he thought about it. Lyndon looked him over, not seeing any resemblance to Levi, and felt his temper rising.

"Did I mess up your boyfriend?" Lyndon sneered, his mind jumping to what he thought was obviously the correct conclusion.

"My *brother*, jackass," the blond sneered back, thumping Lyndon on the chest for emphasis.

*Obviously the incorrect conclusion.* Lyndon's anger dwindled to an ember as he caught the guy's hand before he could smack Lyndon again. "Brother?" was about all he could get out because his heart was thudding rambunctiously, sending just about every bit of blood racing down to fill his cock.

A sharp pain exploding out from his shin did a lot to curb Lyndon's swelling erection. It also almost brought him to his knees, would have except he was shoved forcefully. Lyndon went sprawling backwards on his ass, landing hard enough to jar every bone in his body.

"Yes, my brother! Gah!" Levi's brother bent down and thumped Lyndon's nose for good measure, and Lyndon had had enough.

He grabbed his attacker's wrist and jerked, bringing him down beside Lyndon. All it took was one hand pressed to that thin chest and Lyndon leaning over to growl a warning. The struggling ceased but the anger in those blue eyes amplified and would have burnt Lyndon to a pile of ash in an instant if such a thing were possible.

"I've had enough of your tantrum," Lyndon said after finding enough restraint to keep his voice calm. "Stop trying to hurt me or else I will turn you over my knee." It wouldn't be a bit of fun, either, but Lyndon would damn well do it. "I've never picked on someone smaller than me before—well, I've never picked on anyone, period, but you are sure tempting me every time you try to damage me!"

To his utter horror, Levi's brother's eyes welled and his bottom lip trembled. "Y-you w-wouldn't—"

As a distraction, it worked perfectly, because Lyndon was on the verge of babbling out an apology for being so rough with the guy when a hand landed on his shoulder and Lyndon found himself spun around and dodging a fist. The scent he'd dreamed of for a week hit him more forcefully than the punch he couldn't avoid. Lyndon wound up flat on his back, his head smacking the paved ground and sending bright bursts of light to dance in his vision as a weight settled on his chest. He blinked away the starbursts and struggled when his wrists were grabbed then knelt on.

This put Levi's crotch against Lyndon's chin, and the musky odour of his sexy snow leopard's arousal shot through Lyndon setting him to flame as need erupted inside him. He looked into pale green eyes topped by dark scrunched eyebrows and felt a wave of relief chasing his desire. *Finally!*

"Keep an eye out for anyone coming around, Oscar," the man who'd haunted Lyndon's dreams ordered, and Oscar got up, huffing and glaring but doing as his brother asked.

"Fine, Levi, but if he hurts you again, I'm going to call the taxidermist." Oscar didn't sound like he was joking, either.

*What a vicious little shit. Manipulative, too.* He'd played Lyndon, using those tears and trembling lips. *And I'm an idiot for falling for it, just like I'm an idiot for being unable to look away from those beautiful green eyes —*

"Levi." The name was pulled out of him, torn free even though Lyndon hadn't wanted to speak. But the name had been rolling around in his head for a week. Now it'd plopped down and hit his tongue, and Lyndon hadn't been able to resist saying it.

Levi's mouth, which had been opened to no doubt blast Lyndon with some vitriol or another, snapped shut audibly when Lyndon said Levi's name. Levi moved his hips, his knees grinding against the bones in Lyndon's wrists. The pain there was smothered by the pleasure at Levi's reaction as he rubbed his groin on the underside of Lyndon's chin. It was an instinctive move, all the more sexy for that, but as soon as Levi realised what he was doing, he cursed and scooted back, slapping his hands over Lyndon's wrists at almost the same time he moved his knees off them.

Lyndon's smile was as feral as it had ever been when he narrowed his eyes at Levi. "I could flip you, pin you, fuck you like you wanted—still want," he purred, delighted when Levi shivered and exhaled shakily, his green eyes now almost entirely black as his pupils dilated. "You'd let me. Maybe you'd struggle enough to make me work for it, but not too much." Lyndon could read the want in the man more clearly than he'd ever read anyone. He shifted his arms enough to loosen Levi's hold, then he grabbed his wrists in a swift move that wasn't more than a blur.

"That's what you want, isn't it? A rough, powerful mating, to be claimed and owned and—" Lyndon had to stop—he was so aroused he could hardly breathe. He'd never felt this instinctive need, this instant possessiveness like he felt now. That night in the woods, he'd been freaked and confused and it had still been the hardest thing he'd ever done, leaving Levi behind. The wrongness of his action had eaten at

Lyndon all week, but he'd kept himself from seeking the man out, at least on Levi's property. And considering the way his blond demonic brother was still muttering about taxidermists, that had probably been a wise decision on Lyndon's part.

"What are you? Who are you?" Levi asked in a strangled voice. "How the hell can you know?"

The question cut through the lust strung tight between them and sent a chill over Lyndon's skin. The attraction between them was so strong it almost seemed supernatural. Maybe it was supernatural, what did he know? Not much, but he could answer at least one question before he asked any of his own.

"My name is Lyndon Hines." He kept a visual lock with Levi. "I would ask you the same questions." And he was afraid neither of them was going to have the answers.

# Chapter Seven

"I don't know," Levi admitted, his mind swirling, mixing thoughts of golden hair and eyes, grunts and mewls, the purring sound the man beneath him had made when he'd climaxed. "What are you doing here? Why did you leave—" *me?* Levi shut up, the questions having tumbled out as soon as they'd popped up. But that last one, oh no, it carried too much of the longing and anger Levi had battled against for a week. He'd gone back every night, of course he had, his body aching with a need it knew Lyndon could sate, at least temporarily. Levi had a feeling giving himself over to Lyndon once wouldn't be enough. He'd crave more touches, more rough hands holding him down, more bites and thrusts and—

Lyndon tightened his grip on Levi's wrists. "I don't know why I'm here, it just—it was a place to stop for a while." Lyndon's jaw firmed as he frowned. Levi would bet that wasn't the truth, or at least not all of it. "And, I didn't know what to do. Cougars are territorial. For all I knew, there were more of your kind out there. I didn't expect them to be as accommodating as you."

"As accommodating." Levi twisted his wrists free, not hard to do when Lyndon didn't bother trying to keep him held. "Accommodating." The word hurt like a fired poker through his chest. Levi didn't care to think of himself in such a way, although he supposed it was better than saying he'd begged like a horny slut. *But accommodating? What the fuck?* He was off Lyndon and backing away before Lyndon could even push to his elbows.

Levi kept moving back, stopping only when Oscar's touch prevented him from stumbling over his brother. He looked at the man who made him yearn for things he'd never expected to actually have. It made him ache deep inside, but Levi thought he deserved it for being stupid enough to be tied up in knots over a guy he didn't know and had only rubbed off on. It also pissed him off, because he wasn't some moody, insecure adolescent, yet that was exactly what he'd been acting like over the past week — and it wasn't getting any better.

"Fuck you and your condescending bullshit," Levi growled, more infuriated when he realised his cock was still as hard as a freaking steel pipe. He turned and caught Oscar by the elbow, started dragging him out of the alley — and why the hell was Oscar trying to dig in his heels anyway? Whose side was he on here?

"Stop."

If anyone had told Levi that he'd ever come to heel from one simple, sternly spoken word, he'd have laughed in their face right before he slugged them. Yet his spine snapped straight and his legs followed the command Lyndon uttered even as his mind yelled at him to *movemovemove!* The turmoil between what he wanted to do and what he thought he should do threatened to make him shout in frustration, so Levi pressed his lips together and — stopped, his neck bent as he waited for what.

Beside him, Oscar muttered softly but slid his hand in Levi's and squeezed. "It's fine, it's good he didn't let you walk away — or run away, like he did." Oscar added so much volume to all but the first two words, Levi wouldn't have been surprised if everyone in town had heard him.

"That was a mistake, I admit, and," Levi jumped at the soft caress to his nape, then had to bite his tongue to keep from whimpering when Lyndon dug beneath his collar and scraped his nails over the patch of skin Lyndon had marked. "I'm sorry." He said nothing more, made no promises, but Levi couldn't stop himself from leaning back, just a little, drawing comfort from Lyndon's body heat. "Come with me."

It wasn't really a question so Levi didn't bother answering, he just let his back rest against Lyndon's chest, let Lyndon soothe him using gentle caresses down his side, over his hip, his flank.

Oscar untangled their hands and touched a finger to Levi's chin. Levi blinked at him, trying to decide if he should be embarrassed for turning into such a brainless slut or not, but Oscar's delighted smile took most of the worry from Levi's shoulders.

"I swear, I'll have him stuffed, Levi." Oscar tipped his head enough to glare over Levi's shoulder. Whatever stare-war or pissing match Oscar and Lyndon had, it was brief, with Oscar looking no less fiercely past Levi as he said, "Bring him home. He has orders to finish."

Levi groaned and pinched the bridge of his nose, because God knows that hadn't made him sound like some sort of subby slave something or another. Levi wasn't sure which terms applied, but he was reasonably sure they all started with an 's'. "I'll finish the last chair for the Aberdeen's in the morning, like I said I would." At least it was an explanation of sorts. Didn't make him sound like he came running on command. Oscar was watching him questioningly and Levi smiled a little at his ferociously protective little brother—a side of Oscar he'd not seen often, but then again, when had there been cause?

"Go on, take the truck." He started to dig the keys out of his pocket only to stop when Oscar shook his head.

"Drake will be here to eat at Jambree's," he said, referring to the diner. "I'll catch a ride home with him. Don't want you being stranded." Oscar gave him a quick hug, ignoring Lyndon's hand that still rested on Levi's hip, then he was off, moving in that graceful way he had.

"Your brother is something else."

Levi jerked like he'd stepped barefoot on a livewire. Lyndon's voice, soft and low, his breath warm and moist, all of it against Levi's ear had goose bumps breaking out over his skin.

"Who's Drake?" Lyndon asked, tormenting Levi in the best way, his lips barely brushing Levi's ear. Lyndon trailed his hand down Levi's hip, around to the inside of his thigh where his erection throbbed in the confines of his jeans. He rubbed that length forcefully and Levi couldn't keep back the whimper he'd swallowed down before. It burst free at the first stinging touch.

"'Nother brother," he panted then thumped his head against Lyndon's shoulder. "Stop, please! It's—not while we're talking about my family, okay?"

He thought the vibration against his back was Lyndon chuckling, but since the man didn't make a sound, Levi couldn't be sure. When the movements stopped, though, Lyndon cupped Levi's elbow and stepped beside him. With his other hand, he palmed Levi's chin and tipped it towards him.

"How about we don't talk at all, other than you agreeing to come back to my room? Afterwards you can tell me about your family, if you'd like."

Was that yearning he saw in those golden eyes? Levi wished he knew for sure, but studying them for several seconds didn't clarify it. If Lyndon was wishing he had a family, Levi would gladly give him half of his. Well, maybe a quarter of them. Some of them were beyond being a pain in the ass. Levi opened his mouth to say yes or okay, but what came out made his cheeks flame. "You're not going to run off again after?"

Lyndon arched a dark gold eyebrow. "It's my hotel room, not your private property. But no, I promise." He smiled then, a slick hot twist of lips that Levi would have begged to feel around his cock. "And I'll give you what we both want. I won't leave you wanting again."

*Jesus!* Levi stood debating his options. He wanted what Lyndon was offering—in a way. The idea of being discarded afterwards though, that held no appeal at all and made him hesitate to agree. If he'd been a confused mess after the heated exchange in the woods, what would he feel like after giving himself to Lyndon if the man left again?

Levi grunted to himself, acknowledging the likelihood that he'd not handle that well. It gave him the strength to shake his head and meet that golden stare. "I'll go to the hotel, and we'll talk. That's it."

And God, he hoped he had the fortitude to stick to his words.

Lyndon narrowed his eyes and studied him for a moment before he sighed and ran thick fingers through his sunny blond hair. "All right, if that's what you want. We'll just...talk."

Levi shivered at the rasp in Lyndon's voice. He didn't sound convinced that talking was all that would occur. Levi wasn't convinced himself, but he was damn well going to try not to do anything else stupid. He gestured towards the hotel then walked beside Lyndon, every step leaving Levi feeling as if he was being inexorably drawn to his fate.

# Chapter Eight

*Talk. Just talk.* Lyndon's cougar was throwing a hissy inside, wanting a hell of a lot more than talking, or a lot less. If it were up to his cat, he'd have Levi naked and screaming beneath him as soon as the hotel room door was shut. *It's a good thing I've got more control than my cougar. This is too important to screw up again.* Why that was so, and why this one man called to him so, Lyndon didn't know. He just knew that he couldn't have walked away had his life depended on it.

As they crossed the street, that sensation of being watched returned. Lyndon glanced around and caught a glint of sunlight on pale blond hair. *Oscar, then.* That was all right. He liked that there was someone watching out for Levi, even though he meant to take over that position. First he'd have to convince Levi of that, though. Lyndon knew where Levi's reticence to mate was coming from, or at least he was pretty sure he did. If Lyndon had felt wrecked from abandoning Levi a week ago, how must Levi feel? Judging by his tight jaw and the scent of nervous sweat tinged heavily with arousal, Levi had to be at least as confused as Lyndon. Probably even hurt, which hadn't been Lyndon's intention, but who the hell would have thought a quick one-off would lead to the sort of emotional entanglement that was already growing between them?

Lyndon caught Levi's elbow and almost moaned at the heat seeping through his clothes. He met Levi's gaze and tipped his chin to the left. "It's the last room down this way."

Levi's cautious smile set Lyndon's stomach to fluttering like it had when he'd kissed his first crush years ago. It was sweet and sexy, and Lyndon knew then he was going to find it impossible to leave Levi even if he didn't want Lyndon around.

He slid his hand down Levi's forearm and skimmed his fingers over Levi's palm before letting go of him, conscious of the fact they were in a small town where people might not react well to two men holding hands. His fingers itched to lock with Levi's regardless, so Lyndon stuffed them in his pants pocket and pulled out his wallet to get the key card for the door. That task done, he gave Levi what he hoped was a reassuring smile then started towards his room, gaze sweeping the parking lot to see if anyone was watching. He wouldn't want to cause problems for Levi here.

"Your door is open," Levi said in a barely audible voice. "And I smell cougar — not you."

Lyndon's heart stopped then slammed hard against his ribs as he grabbed Levi's shoulder and squeezed. He saw the slight gap where the hotel room door hadn't quite been shut all the way and cursed himself for thinking he was safe.

"Is there—" Levi sighed and shook his head before darting a glance from Lyndon to the door. "Do you have someone else?"

"No," Lyndon bit out, angry that Levi would think so little of him but more angry at himself for giving Levi reason to do so. Fear also fuelled his temper. He wasn't afraid for himself. Lyndon sniffed the air and barely caught a whiff of the other cougar, but the scent was familiar and his pulse pounded as his two halves had a quick disagreement. His cat wanted to stay and fight and claim Levi as his own, but the man in him wondered if it wouldn't be best to leave and hopefully keep Levi from becoming involved in this twisted game that had become Lyndon's life.

"Don't even think it," Levi growled, and Lyndon looked at him, surprised at Levi's perception. "I can read you—" he faltered, blanching and turning away.

"Great," Lyndon muttered. Now he had another thing to try not to freak out over. *Jesus, what is going on between us? And if he can 'read' me, can I do the same to him?* This wasn't the time to worry about that, but Lyndon did intend to investigate it. Right now he had another question to ask. "How sharp is your sense of smell when you're like this?"

Levi's frown wrinkled his brow in a manner Lyndon found entirely too adorable. "Not as good as when I'm my other, but—" He sniffed. "Good enough to pick up what I should have a few minutes ago if I hadn't been distracted by you." Levi tempered that with a smile that eased away some of Lyndon's tension. "Whoever it was is gone now, and the odour of his markings is very strong. Can't you smell it?"

Lyndon shook his head as Levi fanned a hand under his nose. He was impressed with Levi's abilities. "Not as strong as you can. I don't think I retain as much of my cougar's attributes as you do your snow leopard's." So was he defective, or were their shifter differences normal? Did it matter? Not right then it didn't. "I'm going to go check the room out. Wait—"

"I'm not your little woman," Levi snapped. "I don't need to be protected and I will *not* stand out here like a simpering, brainless idiot while you play the part of the hero. If that's all you think of me..."

Lyndon shut his mouth against a lie claiming Levi had misunderstood. He could no more lie to this man than he could pull the moon down and hold it in his hands. "All right. I'm sorry. I just don't know how to handle all this—all these emotions and instincts I feel when I'm with you." Lyndon contemplated stopping there, but figured he might as well finish what he wanted to say and damn being coy. "Or when I think about you. And I don't want you hurt, okay? I won't apologise for that or try to stop wanting you safe." Any amusement he felt withered as he tipped his head towards the room. "This, it's a threat, a promise. I've been followed for months and I don't know why or by whom."

Levi was looking, slowly moving his eyes across the area, and Lyndon wondered if his vision was sharper than a human's, just like his sense of smell was obviously greater than Lyndon's.

Lyndon retained only a hint of his cougar's senses while in human form. This didn't seem to be the case for Levi, and Lyndon wondered again if there was something wrong with him. Maybe that was why his father had run him off, why another cougar was after him. If his mother had been a cougar, would she have killed him at birth or left him to die because he wasn't as right as nature had intended? Then again, is was also possible he was just whining too much, even if he was keeping it to an internal —

"Stop it," Levi said, touching Lyndon's hip. "You're giving me a headache from all the worrying about whatever it is that's on your mind. I don't see anyone watching, and I'm fairly certain the other shifter isn't in your room. The scent isn't fresh, though it's only a couple of hours old. Shall we check it out?"

"Yeah," Lyndon muttered, a little stunned because he could still only detect the other cougar's scent faintly, much less put it down to a time and level of 'freshness'. He started towards the room again and once they reached the door, he couldn't stop himself from placing a hand on Levi's shoulder. "I know you aren't a wuss or whatever, but can you let me go in first? I can't shake this instinct that says I have to protect you. It—" He pressed his other hand to his stomach, pushed hard enough to make himself grunt. "It's like a knot here, burning and I just can't ignore it."

Levi's expression remained blank, but something in his eyes softened, looked less chilled. He touched Lyndon's stomach and it Lyndon's knees weak. "Okay, but I am going to be right on your heels." He stroked Lyndon's belly through his shirt, distracting him for a second as want spiralled down to his groin. Levi smiled crookedly and pulled his hand back. "After you."

Lyndon willed back the cloud of need and turned to the door. The odour was stronger, burning his nostrils as he pushed the door open and surveyed the small room. "At least he didn't wreck it," he murmured. Except for the dresser drawers being open and his clothes piled onto the bed, nothing was out of place. Lyndon sighed and walked in, Levi so close behind him he smacked against Lyndon's back when he stopped.

Now Lyndon could detect the pungent aroma, could pick out the hours it had taken to saturate the air. "He's gone," he said, craning his neck to get a glimpse into the bathroom. He pushed the door open and flinched when he saw a hint of his reflection in the mirror above the bathroom sink.

*A little jumpy, dumbass?* The shower curtain was pulled back. There was nowhere else someone could have been hiding in there. It was also obvious to his senses that he and Levi were the only two people in the place.

Levi exhaled, his breath wafting over the back of Lyndon's neck and drawing goose bumps up on his skin. Lyndon started to reach for him but Levi moved around to the bed and poked at the pile of clothes. He wrinkled his nose in away Lyndon found endearing. "This stuff is rank. What kind of jerk *sprays* like a wild cat? It's just a nasty thing to do."

"At least that's all he did this time," Lyndon muttered, thinking of the other ways the cougar shifter had made his presence known before. "Let's just say this guy lets his cat have its way when it comes to marking his territory."

Levi glanced up at him and frowned. "This isn't his territory, though. You're the first cougar shifter I've ever met—the first of any other kind of shifter I've ever met—and I've lived here all my life. If anything, this would be your territory, except," Levi shot him a wicked smile, "it already belongs to a family of snow leopards."

Obviously Lyndon's cougar wasn't as territorial as Lyndon had feared, because Levi's proclamation didn't make his cat protest. Instead his cougar purred and pushed to touch, so Lyndon did, reaching out to trace the smile on Levi's lips, first using a finger followed by the tip of his tongue as Lyndon cupped Levi's nape.

Levi opened for him beautifully, his lips parting and his tongue following Lyndon's lead. A soft mewling sound bled from Levi and Lyndon swallowed the sound then pulled Levi closer. Levi rested his hands on Lyndon's hips, not holding, just touching, and writhed against him in a way that threatened to demolish Lyndon's restraint. The urge to push Levi down and take him here, to fill the room with the scent of their mating instead of the offensive odour of the other cougar was so overwhelming it caused Lyndon to jerk back and stumble. He caught himself by grabbing onto the bed and glanced at Levi as they both panted.

"Come back to my place," Levi rasped, looking a little stunned as soon as he said it. Then he forged on before Lyndon could figure out a response. "This room is vile, and even if Oscar comes and helps us clean it, you at least will still be able to detect the other cougar's scent. And he knows where you are—"

That snapped Lyndon to and he straightened up while anger set a pounding off in his temple. "Which means he will only find me again. I don't think you'd want Oscar endangered, or yourself."

Levi tilted his head to the side, his auburn hair brushing over his shoulder as he slowly grinned. "It's sweet, you being worried, but you misunderstand. It's not just Oscar there. Four of my five siblings live on the property as well, as do my parents and grandparents. Trust me when I say that anyone who fucks with Grandma Marybeth is going to end up in bloody pieces on the ground. She's the reason my family is here. Originally Marybeth lived in the Himalayas..." Levi trailed off, a rosy colour tinting his cheeks.

Lyndon didn't know what to say. He suspected he wanted Levi more than just physically, and the idea of a home, a family, caused the yearning Lyndon tried to keep buried to rise to the surface and throb like a living, breathing thing. Levi seemed to take his silence for acquiescence, and Lyndon couldn't find it in himself to protest when Levi kept talking.

"Chances are, anyway, whoever this is will have seen us together, or will catch my scent if he returns. He could be watching the room now. I'd think he would be, even though I didn't see anyone. There are lots of places to hide. My point is, he'd find me anyway, and wouldn't you rather us be together if he did find me?"

Lyndon wasn't sure if Levi was trying to convince him or both of them, but the point sunk in and hit its intended target. "All right, I'll come."

Levi's relief was palpable, and those pale eyes crinkled around the edges as he smiled. "Okay, okay that's good. You can tell me more about yourself and whatever you know about the weirdo who did this. Maybe we can figure out what's going on—and we can ask Oscar. He's really smart." Levi grimaced and looked around the room. "And good at cleaning. Mind if I call him and ask him to come lend a hand?"

"As long as he doesn't attack me and have me stuffed," Lyndon groused. This wasn't going to endear him to Oscar, and Lyndon knew Levi and Oscar were close. He'd rather not get any further on Oscar's bad side. He really thought Oscar was okay. Kind of cute in a possessed crazy terrier way, at least when it came to his brother. Lyndon thought they'd get along just fine, eventually, if he worked hard at getting Oscar to like him—and if he didn't run again.

# Chapter Nine

Levi wasn't surprised at all when Lyndon kicked the cabin door shut with his heel before pinning Levi against the wall. The tension in the truck on the drive home had been so thick it had practically weighted the air, and despite both men's claim that they would talk, this was exactly what Levi had been hoping would happen. He didn't think he could concentrate on a conversation when he was burning up with desire.

His back hit the wall hard enough to knock the breath from his lungs, then Lyndon was on him, pressed so tightly to him Levi could feel Lyndon's heart beating a rapid staccato.

"We'll talk later, much later," Lyndon growled right before crushing Levi's lips under his.

Levi's mind shorted out and hot spikes of need shot to his dick. Lyndon wedged a hand between them and cupped Levi's balls, giving them a squeeze that had Levi's ass clenching. He looped his arms around Lyndon's shoulders, grabbing his shirt and rending seams. His mouth was plundered, Lyndon claiming every bit of it using forceful sweeps of his tongue.

"*He'll* talk now, before he mauls my grandson anymore. There are just some things a grandma shouldn't see."

Levi yelped and banged his head on the wall. Lyndon cursed and stumbled back, swinging around to where Grandma Marybeth stood in the kitchen doorway. Levi couldn't look away from Lyndon's mouth, his lips rosy and wet from their kiss, parted while he panted, much like Levi was doing.

"Who are you?" Lyndon asked then closed his eyes and snorted. "Stupid question. Marybeth, right?"

Levi had filled Lyndon in on who was who in his family during the time they were working on cleaning the hotel room, which still stank to high heaven in his opinion. If he had his way, Lyndon wouldn't be returning there. Wouldn't be leaving, either.

Marybeth, all five-foot-two of her, gave Lyndon a look that should have scorched the skin right off him. "And you're Lyndon Hines. At least you aren't stupid. Oscar had his doubts. Oscar's a good boy. He told me what happened as soon as he and Drake got back."

And a bit of tattling was what Levi got for not insisting Oscar hang around and wait for them to finish up the room. Instead, Levi had agreed it would be best to let Oscar ride with Drake since their other brother was in town.

"Oscar." Levi closed his eyes as he slumped against the wall. Right now it was all that was holding him up. The sudden switch from being wildly aroused to not, courtesy of his grandmother's appearance, had sapped the strength from his body. He slid down the wall anyway, grunting as he landed on his butt. "I'm going to strangle Oscar."

Lyndon's sharp laughter had Levi snapping his eyes open and glaring at him. Lyndon shook his head and casually leaned on the back of the couch. "He's just watching out for you."

"As am I," Marybeth said, walking over to stand beside Levi. "Get up. You're not some wilting flower type."

Cheeks burning, Levi did as he was told, averting his face from Lyndon.

Marybeth patted his back then nudged him. "Have a seat. You too," she added to Lyndon.

Both men sat on the couch, Lyndon unhesitatingly placing his hand on Levi's knee as he watched Marybeth. She had greying hair and soft features, and should have appeared grandmotherly. Instead she reminded Levi of a leopardess protecting her young. Her grey eyes glowed, a fierceness in their depths that was almost tangible, and her rounded, wrinkled face seemed to sharpen, giving her the look of a huntress after prey. She studied Lyndon for a full minute then sat back in her chair gracefully, like a queen reclining on her throne.

"Cougar, Oscar said." She cut her eyes at Levi and let him know in one quick glance she wasn't happy with him "Since Levi didn't seem to think it important to inform me about his...encounter you two had a week ago, you get to answer all the questions."

Lyndon settled into the cushions, leaning back and pulling Levi closer to his side. It was weird to be cuddling in front of his grandma, but Levi wasn't about to protest. Not when Lyndon felt so right beside him.

"I would think Levi had a good reason for not telling you about our 'encounter'. Most grandkids wouldn't run to their grandmothers and tell them about their sex life, would they? Especially not if it involved a nameless stranger and a down and dirty roll in the woods."

If he'd said it to shock Marybeth, he hadn't succeeded. Levi didn't think that was the case, anyway. He'd realised he could kind of pick up Lyndon's moods, little flashes of what he felt though not exactly thoughts. More like impressions, maybe. All he was getting from Lyndon now was the desire to get this conversation over with. And to get Levi under him.

"Jesus," Levi whispered, nestling closer to Lyndon.

Lyndon tightened his arm around Levi and cupped the back of his head, burying his fingers in Levi's hair—which shouldn't have turned him on, but damn it, everything about Lyndon turned him on! Levi shifted on the couch, hoping his erection wouldn't be evident, but one glance at Marybeth and he knew better. She would easily scent every odour in the air, including his arousal. And Lyndon's, which hadn't faded much at all.

"Regardless, Levi, you should have told us there was another shifter on the property. We didn't even know there were other kinds, although I'm not surprised."

Levi started to answer, to apologise, but Marybeth waved him off. "We are, unfortunately, rather ignorant about shifters in a way. My entire pack was murdered, killed for their fur and probably their organs as well. I had been left behind in the huts where we lived as humans. If one of the hunters hadn't found me and thought me to be an abandoned child, I would have died too."

Levi had known that much about his grandmother's past. He couldn't imagine being raised by the very people who had slaughtered your family, but he understood Marybeth hadn't had any other option. She refused to talk about her childhood spent with the hunters. As far as she seemed concerned, her life during that time didn't exist, like she was in an odd sort of stasis until she'd met Grandpa Vincent.

"All the knowledge of who and what we are died with my father, who was the story teller—historian, I suppose he'd be called in human terms." She sighed and rubbed at the pleat in her purple trousers. "There's very little I remember. I don't recall him mentioning other shifters. I do know the gene for shifting is passed down from mother to child, so only the females can propagate our species. Is it the same for cougars?"

Lyndon had gone tense beside him at the question. Levi lifted his head from Lyndon's shoulder and debated asking why he felt anger coming from the man.

"No, it's paternal for us, and I've never heard of any cougars living together like your family did in the Himalayas, or here, even as humans. We seem to be as solitary as the actual cats." He paused and darted a glance at Levi. "Although there was a cougar shifter who took me in and helped me out after my mom died. Grady made sure I was taken care of, and he didn't ask anything in return. He didn't know me, didn't owe me anything either, but I don't know if he was the exception to the rule or if most cougar shifters are just like regular folks. Some good, some bad."

Marybeth narrowed her eyes and smiled thinly. "And yet, here you sit, snuggling alongside my grandson and all but growling over him. What would you say, Lyndon, if I told you to leave? If I made you leave?"

"Grandma—" Levi began, panic wedging in his heart.

Lyndon soothed him slightly, caressing his nape and murmuring softly.

"I'd say it wasn't your choice, Marybeth." Lyndon lightly scratched at Levi's neck, unerringly finding the spot he'd marked. It still bore the faint pattern of his teeth. "I'd say..." Lyndon's breath stuttered as he exhaled, was steady when he inhaled. He relaxed beside Levi, and his voice was laced with surety when he next spoke. "I'd say it's Levi's decision, and mine. Not yours. And if he wanted me to leave"—Lyndon used his other hand to frame Levi's face and tip his head back slightly—"I'd do whatever I could to convince him to come with me or let me stay." Lyndon appeared to be surprised by his own words, his eyes wide and slightly panicked looking.

Levi was, and by the truth he sensed in the statement. Marybeth said something, but Levi wasn't listening to her, he was listening to his body, his leopard, both of which were telling him he needed to feel Lyndon's lips on his more than he needed his heart to keep beating.

Lyndon's mouth curved into a smile that set Levi's body to tingling, then he kissed Levi, holding him in place as Lyndon thrust his tongue into Levi's eager mouth.

When Lyndon lifted his head, Levi felt dizzy and breathless, his lips hyper-sensitive and swollen. He wanted to taste Lyndon again, to drown in his flavours, but Marybeth's 'ahem' stopped him from begging Lyndon for more. He turned at his grandma in a sort of daze. One side of her mouth quirked up in a grin as she steepled her fingers together under her chin. Lyndon was tightly wound beside him, on the verge, no doubt, of throwing Levi over the coffee table and fucking him regardless of who was there.

"I may know what's going on here," Marybeth murmured, seeming to grow more pleased the longer she stared at them. Levi just felt horny and anxious for her to leave already. "I wasn't sure if I was misremembering since it didn't happen to me, or my children. Or maybe it's because you're both shifters, I just don't know, but..." she shrugged and pushed herself up from the chair, and Levi knew from the devilish glint to her eyes, she wasn't going to fill them in on her epiphany. "I need to think about this." The look she pinned on Lyndon would have had Levi cringing, but he didn't so much as blink. "You and I aren't done."

"We are for now," Lyndon replied, then Levi was on his back and Lyndon was covering him from chest to thigh, kissing him until all Levi could taste was this one man, all he could hear or feel was Lyndon. Levi didn't even hear his grandmother's laughter or the slamming of the front door except as a kind of echo, faint and almost nonsensical to his fevered mind. Then Lyndon bit his bottom lip, and Levi didn't think about anything at all except the man who'd owned him since the moment their eyes had met in the forest.

# Chapter Ten

Talking to Marybeth had left Lyndon with more questions than answers, but he'd deal with those questions later. For now, he had his man beneath him, writhing and moaning and enticing Lyndon more every second.

Lyndon noted Levi's reaction when he had bitten his lip. Levi hadn't responded as much to the scrape of teeth, but an actual bite, the breaking of skin just enough to get a coppery hint of flavour, set Levi off, pulling sweet monas from him. Much more of it and Levi would probably blow. Lyndon didn't want him to, not yet. He wanted to feel Levi come from the inside out.

"Come on, I need more room than we have on this couch to fuck you the way we both want me to." Lyndon stood, tugging an eager Levi up too. He placed his hand on Levi's nape when he started to take a step. Levi shuddered and turned hungry green eyes to him. "Strip first. I've thought of seeing you naked and needing since the moment I first saw you."

"Fuck," Levi whispered before dropping his gaze down. His fingers shook badly as he tried to unbutton his denim shirt and Lyndon reached out to help him, only to fumble the buttons, too.

Levi muttered and Lyndon cursed, then Lyndon grabbed the open neck of the shirt and jerked, sending buttons flying and pinging across the room. He stripped the shirt off in one harsh tug, groaning at the sight of Levi's furry chest.

Lyndon stroked the dark pelt then scraped his nails over Levi's nipples. Levi mewled and caught Lyndon's wrists, holding his hands still.

"Please," Levi asked, leaning into Lyndon's touch. "More."

"Whatever you need," Lyndon rasped, finding the hard nubs and pinching them.

"Oh!" Levi clawed at Lyndon's hands, pushing them against his nipples. "Harder!"

Lyndon purred, there was no other word for it. His cock leaked in his excitement as he dipped his head and bit one coral tip while he twisted the other. Levi cried out and the sharp tang of cum flooded the air between them. Lyndon bit his nipple reprovingly even as he revelled in having brought Levi to release.

"Have to teach you some control," he murmured before nudging Levi back on the couch. Lyndon forgot about his plans to make it to the bedroom as he loved on Levi's nipples, soaking in his whimpers and gasps.

The little nubs were red and swollen, Levi's chest marked by teeth and nails when Lyndon fisted his hands in Levi's hair and devoured his mouth. Levi undulated beneath him, his cock hard again. Lyndon claimed every bit of Levi his tongue could reach, then bit at his lips until Levi whined and pleaded for more.

Only then did Lyndon slide down his body and torment his nipples again.

Lyndon's cock was so hard he couldn't breathe without it hurting. He sat up and grabbed the waistband of Levi's jeans. The wet spot there was too tempting to resist, so Lyndon didn't bother trying. He bent and licked it, moaning as his first taste of Levi's cum flooded his sense.

"Off, goddamn it," he growled, jerking at the stubborn fastening of the jeans.

Levi cursed and muttered for Lyndon to get up. Grudgingly, painfully thanks to his dick, Lyndon did so and Levi got the jeans undone and started removing them Lyndon watched impatiently until he realised Levi still had his boots on. Lyndon tugged them off then finished divesting Levi of his jeans. He stripped rapidly, unconcerned about buttons or seams, his need fuelled by the hunger in Levi's eyes as the man watched him remove his clothes.

Lyndon grinned as he fisted the base of his dick. He'd never had a complaint about its size—at least, not any he'd consider a negative complaint. Levi's eyes were about to bug out of his head, and the scent of fear mingled with the stronger one of arousal. Lyndon stopped stroking himself as he studied Levi. He hated having to ask, because he was kind of scared of the answer, but he needed to know.

"You've done this before—bottomed?"

Levi gulped and turned a shade of red Lyndon hadn't seen before. "Uh. Once? When—when I was a kid, my first kind of boyfriend was afraid to bottom so I did instead. It, ah, didn't go so well."

Lyndon arched an eyebrow, his curiosity holding back the urge to pounce for now. "Could you explain what happened in more detail?" The last thing he wanted to do was repeat the 'kind of boyfriend's' mistakes. Reminding himself that Levi had probably had a lover as young and inexperienced as himself back then didn't really help. Lyndon wanted to find the guy and slap some love-making skills into him.

Levi blushed from his thighs to his ears, but he kept his eyes on Lyndon's. "Well, it wasn't really Yancy's fault." Lyndon tried not to scoff, but *Yancy? Who the fuck named their kid Yancy?*

"He was really a bottom, you know. I kind of begged and nagged and...I pushed when I shouldn't have, but I was young and impatient and I wanted to know what it felt like to get fucked since Yancy sure as hell enjoyed it."

Levi shrugged. "I think he only agreed because he was afraid he'd have to go back to beating off if he didn't. All I can do is guess about why he said he'd try, but he didn't want to, I can tell now when I remember it all. Plus, apparently he couldn't remember all the effort I put into making sure he was ready. But Yancy was just one of those guys who was sweet and kinda, uh, kind of dumb. No common sense but really smart book-wise. He moved away with his folks not too long after that."

Lyndon decided not to push for more details. He was pretty sure he got it. "So you topped only afterwards."

Levi picked at a spot on the couch, pulling on a thread. "I haven't been with a lot of guys — and no girls, before you ask — "

Lyndon hadn't been fixing to ask. He knew Levi was gay, same as him.

"After Yancy, it was a couple years. Then only some hook-ups when I'd get to Aspen or Denver, somewhere like that." Levi waved a hand in front of his chest. "All those guys, they took a look at me and figured I was a top, and I dunno, maybe I was for them. It sounds bad, but I just needed someone and if it meant fucking when I was kind of wanting to be fucked instead, well, I settled for what was offered. Besides, I wasn't sure I wanted one of those guys to do me." Levi's lopsided grin did funny things to Lyndon's insides. "I was afraid they'd be as bad at it as Yancy had been."

"Okay, enough about Yancy and other men." Lyndon watched Levi's flush deepening as Levi's lashes swept his cheeks. "Come here."

"I feel like a yo-yo with all this up and down stuff," Levi grumbled.

Lyndon grunted and enjoyed the way Levi's abs rippled and his cock bobbed as he stood. Lyndon stepped back and studied Levi for a moment, from his shaggy auburn hair past shy eyes and glistening lips, to his broad thickly muscled shoulders. Firm pecs and ridged stomach, long, defined arms and thighs, dark hair covering them like a pelt. Levi's waist was narrow, his hips lean, but it was the dense bush and jutting dick drawing Lyndon's attention again and again. Well, and the heavy sac hanging beneath, fuzzed and tempting.

Seeing no reason to resist, Lyndon cupped Levi's balls and rolled them as Levi's lids drooped and a soft moan escaped his lips.

"Like that?" he asked, applying a slow, steady pressure.

Levi had responded eagerly to a bit of pain. Lyndon needed to know if there were lines he couldn't cross.

"Yes," Levi hissed, bringing his hands up to clutch at Lyndon's shoulders. The sharp bite of his nails was a demand for more, as was the smell of Levi's pre-cum.

"You like this," Lyndon reiterated, tightening his grip. He wanted complete clarification for both of them. "I want to be certain you're enjoying everything we do together."

Levi cracked open his eyes and nibbled on his bottom lip before nodding. "I didn't know I would. I f-fantasised so much but you — ah!" He tipped his head back and shuddered, coming up on his toes as Lyndon applied slightly more pressure to his balls. "Please, fuck me!"

Lyndon released Levi's balls and thought of how he'd had to restrain himself when having sex with a human. The cougar's urge to claw and bite had always been there, a rough edge Lyndon had kept buried because he'd known how fragile people were. Sure there were BDSM clubs and ways to find men who wanted to be hurt, but what was inside of Lyndon wasn't like what drove men in those places. He wasn't a Dom. He was a cougar shifter, and his animal's desires mixed with his human's when it came to pleasure. The idea of not having to hold back when he and Levi fucked was an amazing lure, one that snapped the restraint he had always employed before. His fingers and gums tingled and ached as if he were shifting. A flick of his tongue and a curl of his fist told him some parts of him were already were.

"Are you sure you want me?" he asked in an effort to give Levi an out. Lyndon bared his teeth and uncurled his fist, raising his hand to show both himself and Levi the black claws extending from his fingers. They were short but sharp, and if he hadn't been so horny he thought he'd die from it, he'd have been freaked by it since this had never happened before.

Levi gave him a heavy-lidded glance, a rumbling purr building in his chest as he took one of Lyndon's hands in his. When Levi licked the pointed tip of one nail, it was Lyndon who shook all the way down to his toes. "Yes," Levi murmured. "Please, yes! Mark me—"

Whatever else he was going to say was cut off in a gasp when Lyndon spun him around and shoved him onto the couch. "On your knees, arms braced on top of the couch," he growled.

Levi scrambled, arching his back in a way that spread his rounded ass and gave Lyndon a view of his fluttering hole and swinging balls.

"Mount me," Levi urged, rolling his hips. "Fuck me!"

Lyndon heard the rip of material, saw Levi's hands were curled, short, sharp black nails tearing into the couch. He shot a startled glance at Levi's face, found him peering back over his shoulder, his canines long and deadly points.

He didn't know what exactly was happening here, except it was irresistible. Levi was irresistible. Lyndon picked up his jeans and took out a condom, glad he'd thought to put some in his pocket back in the hotel room. He cursed when he realised what he'd forgotten.

"Lube!" The snarled word was nearly unintelligible. Lyndon's tongue felt thick, his mouth dry. He wanted to bite, to let Levi's blood saturate his parched mouth.

Levi groaned and writhed, arching his back and swaying his hips. "Bedroom, on the nightstand or maybe the floor if—"

Lyndon ran, as uncomfortable as it was. He found the bedroom by following the strongest scent of Levi. The lube wasn't on the nightstand, and he didn't see it on the floor, so he ended up on his knees peeking under the bed. Of course it was there, on the far side beneath the bed. Lyndon was never so grateful for having a long reach as he was just then. He got the lube and quickly dashed back into the living room.

Only to find Levi panting as he worked his dick in long strokes. Lyndon's body tightened at the sight, want prickling all over his skin. He ripped open the package and rolled the condom down his cock, pumping his length once as he considered his options—pounce or draw this sexual tension out until it was so taut it'd snap like a piece of over-stretched barbed wire.

Eyes narrowing, he sought Levi's gaze. A thrill shot through him when the leopard shifter whimpered and stopped jostling his arm. "You shouldn't have started without me."

# Chapter Eleven

The low, rumbled reprimand hit Levi like an erotic punch, need so intense it hurt lighting up his body. He opened his mouth to beg, plead for Lyndon to fuck him, but the sharp slap of palm to ass startled a yelp out of him. The stinging pain added to the fire already burning in him, and Levi spread his legs. He pushed his ass up and received another blow that jostled his cock and balls.

What would happen if he came again? Lyndon had already said something about Levi's lack of control. Before he could decide if he should tell Lyndon to give him a minute to get it together, Lyndon landed a slap to his butt that made Levi scream as he tried to keep from coming. He was so close to climaxing, so, so close—

"No."

Just one word. The power in it had Levi clamping every muscle in his body to keep from spewing. His ass was burning deliciously, his balls drawn tight in an instant. Levi bit his tongue then groaned when the pain only heightened his arousal.

"You'll come when I tell you," Lyndon snapped. Levi mewled, sounding pitiful to his own ears. The feel of cool liquid hitting the top of his crease shut off the pleas which had been on his bleeding tongue.

"You'll wait until I'm buried balls deep in here," Lyndon said, sliding his fingers down the furrow between Levi's cheeks.

The first touch of sharp nails against his hole had Levi crying out and arching for more.

"Be good and I'll fuck you soon," Lyndon purred.

The tip of one finger breached Levi's opening and he froze, afraid to beg or move or do anything that would cause Lyndon to make him wait.

"Just perfect, so fucking perfect. Take what I give you." Lyndon smoothed a hand over Levi's flank then up to his lower back, where he rubbed while slipping his finger in deep. "That will be my dick soon, stretching your tight little hole." He thrust in and out then touched the hidden spot inside Levi he'd heard his past lover's beg him to peg.

"Oh my fucking hell." Levi gasped when ecstasy shot up from his ass. "Oh!"

"Better keep yourself from coming," Lyndon said, sounding strained as Levi's hole burned around a broader intrusion.

Another finger, he thought, not as big as Lyndon's monster cock, and damn, it felt good! Levi panted and struggled to keep still, then finally had to grab his cock and pinch the head hard. A mistake, he realised, teetering closer to the brink. Only the desire to please Lyndon kept Levi from tumbling over.

"Good, you're doing so good."

Lyndon rubbed Levi's spot again and he screamed, need and frustration so tangled with pleasure he could hardly stand it. More burning, stretching, then Lyndon growled and the cushions dipped.

"Now, *now* I'm going to fuck you."

Levi whimpered when the blunt tip of Lyndon's cock penetrated his hole. Then he yowled like the snow leopard he was at times, when Lyndon's thick length speared into his ass.

Lyndon roared, a human shout and cougar's scream combined, and slammed his cock in balls deep. He dropped down on top of Levi, teeth scraping his nape. Lyndon grabbed Levi at hip and shoulder, curling his fingers, his nails marking him. The pain that blossomed from the penetration melded with the pain and pleasure spreading up from his ass, and the sounds Levi loosed left his throat raw.

"Yes," Lyndon grunted. "Mine!" Then he bit, hard and deep, taking Levi over completely, fucking him using short, deep strokes serving to ram Levi's cock against the couch.

Friction and pain, fucking, biting, clawing—Levi's mind spun and splintered from the waves of pleasure rolling over and through him. He snarled, reaching back and digging his nails into Lyndon's thigh, dragging them up to clasp and scratch his pumping ass.

"Fucking hell, yes!" Lyndon lifted his mouth long enough to say, then searing pain highlighted the euphoria when Lyndon bit him again.

"Guh!" Levi had meant to say something, praise or plea or whatever he could get out.

Lyndon drove into him so deep Levi thought he'd never be empty again, and words evaporated in a strangled sound. His cock was getting almost enough friction, almost enough—he was so close, and the way Lyndon was managing to rub the place inside his ass was driving Levi insane. He needed to come, needed more.

Lyndon growled, his teeth sinking deeper at the same time his nails and cock speared Levi. Levi cried out and jerked. Fiery trails were scratched into his skin, down his side, his hip, his thigh while Lyndon battered into him. Levi clenched his ass and a rapturous sensation swam into his veins, making him light-headed.

"More," he thought he managed to gasp, then his dick was taken in a rough, harsh grasp and everything inside him collided and burst into brilliant streams of colour and pleasure so intense, then Lyndon murmured, "Come."

Levi couldn't hold back any longer. He screamed, shredding, clawing whatever he could reach, mindless in his climax. His cock jerked and spunk shot from his slit. Lyndon's shout joined his, and even in the middle of orgasming, Levi felt Lyndon's cock swell and pulse.

"Yes, Levi, fuck," Lyndon groaned, his hips slapping Levi's ass in a scattered rhythm. "So tight, hot—" Lyndon broke off, his strokes to Levi's dick almost spastic by then.

Levi came and came, matching the cock in his ass, filling him back up for each spurt he let loose.

When Lyndon finally stilled, panting and gasping, Levi tried to stay awake. His body ached in so many pleasurable ways, sated as it'd never been before. They needed to talk, needed to do—so many things. Soft wet kisses along his shoulders then up his neck convinced Levi they could talk later. For now he wanted to lie here boneless and quivery, and enjoy the attentions of the man he intended to keep.

# Chapter Twelve

Levi was thoroughly fucked out and Lyndon pretty much the same, and it made it difficult for Lyndon to get up. His cock was still wedged in the tight confines of Levi's body, still enjoying the fluttering spasms of Levi's inner muscles. Lyndon kissed the spot he'd marked. He leaned up to see it and his stomach plummeted even as his cat purred its approval. The mark was large, brutal-looking. Blood seeped from the wounds Lyndon's teeth had made. Tenderly, he bent and lapped at the coppery liquid, his cock twitching at Levi's taste. Sweet, salty, strong — much like the man, Lyndon suspected. Levi was an incredible lover, demanding and so very responsive. He'd begged for more, wanted not only Lyndon's cock, but his bite and scratches.

Lyndon had gone wild on Levi, and Levi had marked him as well. Lyndon's thigh felt like it was on fire, as did his ass cheek. If he was aching, how must Levi feel? Lyndon started to pull back. Levi grumbled a protest and Lyndon traced a hand up Levi's sweaty side — sweaty and bloody, he realised when he reached Levi's biceps. Concern bubbled over into stark worry and regret.

"Levi, come on. I need to see how bad I fucked up. I don't—I didn't mean to—" He'd lost his goddamned mind that was what had happened. Levi had been every fantasy Lyndon had ever had, brought to sheer, screaming, needy life.

And Lyndon had let go. Sure, Levi had urged him on, but the man couldn't have had any idea of what Lyndon would do to him. Lyndon hadn't known he was being so...so violent. He'd only heard his cougar screaming for its—Lyndon shied away from finishing the thought. As far as he knew, cougars didn't have mates, not permanent ones. Yet the word suited, and he didn't feel like he wanted to let Levi go, ever. What the hell was happening here?

"Stop worrying, Christ," Levi muttered. "You're going to suffocate me with your regret and all kinds of crap I don't want."

Lyndon stood and nearly stumbled. His legs were wobbly, which might have been funny had he not almost collapsed. Levi rolled onto his back, hissing when his weight came down on his ass. A beatific smile spread his lips and he turned his sated gaze to Lyndon.

"You gave me exactly what I wanted, Lyndon." Levi let him process the statement, hoping Lyndon would hear the truth in his words. "I've dreamt of being taken just like you did, of having a man bring me pleasure and pain. It—you—are incredible. So please, stop thinking you made a mistake. It does both of us a disservice."

"But—" Lyndon took in the scratches, some deep, others not more than pink trails. Those would surely fade before tomorrow, the light ones, but the others...

"Levi, look at you! You've got scratches and I bit you! Not like before, but bit you and had your blood, your flesh, in my mouth, on my tongue! How can being treated like a scratching post not make you feel like I abused you?"

Levi opened his eyes wide enough to let Lyndon see them roll. "Please. Lyndon. You think it's abuse, giving me what I begged for? And I begged, didn't I? For more, even. I marked you." Levi pointed to the wounds he'd left on Lyndon. "And I knew you liked it. I could feel it, just as I could feel the thrill it gave you to make me yours." Levi tipped his chin up and Lyndon couldn't have looked away from those pale eyes if his life had depended on it. "I am—yours. You know it in here." He leant forward and pressed a hand to Lyndon's chest. "Listen to what you feel here, not the human babbling bullshit in your head. Look at me, know me. I'm yours."

He said it with such conviction, and such devotion, Lyndon almost couldn't grasp it. He'd wondered what was happening between them, but that word, mate, kept swirling around his head, and every time Levi said he belonged to Lyndon, the word grew louder, more insistent. He wished he knew what Levi was thinking, what he was feeling. Levi seemed to be able to peer into him. All Lyndon had to go on was Levi's expressions, his scents.

*And his actions, his words. Do I really need to read his mind or whatever it is he can do to me? Is it necessary when the man is so open and honest already?* No, it wasn't.

"You are," Lyndon said when Levi started to look crestfallen. "You are, and I'm yours. I don't understand how." *Mate!* The nagging word would not desist. Levi smiled slyly and Lyndon wondered if the man heard the same word bouncing around his brain. "And you're sure you're okay? I wasn't too rough?"

Levi stood and hooked a hand around the back of Lyndon's neck, pulling him down the couple of inches necessary for their lips to meet. The kiss was sweet, and Lyndon closed his eyes to enjoy the gift his mate — *there it is again* — was giving him.

"You were perfect," Levi said a bit sluggishly. "I want that again, and again. I want..." Levi moved closer until he was all but glued to Lyndon. Dark need clouded Levi's features as he massaged Lyndon's neck. "More, sometimes. I want to try other things I've thought about."

*Fuck!* Lyndon had to close his eyes before he did something isane like pushing Levi down and fucking him raw...which he probably already was, considering the way Lyndon had just pounded away at his ass.

"Shower," he said in something a hair less embarrassing than a squeak. "Let's get cleaned up, then maybe..." Lyndon took Levi's cock in a firm hold, enjoying the way the soft flesh began to harden in his hand. "Maybe I'll suck this dry." He added a little twist of his wrist, drawing a delicious moan from Levi. Lyndon let go and tried not to look smug. "Lead the way." He'd take the opportunity to watch Levi's tight ass flex.

Which is what he tried to do, but Levi, pride in his voice, pointed out the golden pine floors he'd helped lay, and the matching trim around the doorways and running parallel to the ceiling. A shelf above the fireplace brought a glow of pride to Levi.

Lyndon wanted to devour him right then but turned instead and looked at the detailed carvings on the supporting brackets. Leopards, playing, sleeping, carved with such intricate skill it left him breathless. Gorgeous, but he thought it needed a cougar in the mix now. He'd suggest one later, when he and Levi knew each other better.

"And the kitchen table and chairs, I made those too," Levi went on, veering into the kitchen. "It took me a couple of months working around other orders, but it's exactly what I'd wanted. What do you think?"

Levi wasn't fishing for compliments on his woodworking skills. The man was talented, as much an artist as there ever was. The table was long, claw-footed—leopard paws, of course. The warm honey colour of the wood seemed to welcome one to sit in the high-backed chairs cushioned in colourfully padded material. "It's gorgeous," Lyndon murmured, seeing Levi's touch in the way the counters matched the table, the colour of which in turn blended perfectly with the sills around the windows. The cream-coloured walls offset the wood in a way that would make an interior decorator envious.

"This is what you do? Make these beautiful pieces of furniture for people?"

Levi's shy smile was priceless. "Yeah, and sometimes, if I feel like it, I make other things too." Levi gestured behind Lyndon, who turned and only then noticed the large carved leopard beside the hallway. "I don't sell my cats, though. Those are gifts for family."

Lyndon walked over to the wooden cat and caressed the smooth skull. "It's you, isn't it?"

Levi cleared his throat and Lyndon looked at him, surprised to find the man grimacing.

"Carving an effigy of myself seems vain, right? But it isn't. I had to practice first, and I figured I'd rather botch myself, you know. Silly, maybe, but it seemed disrespectful to try to make one of my grandma and end up making her look like a deformed house cat or something."

"I don't think it's vain, or silly," Lyndon said, smiling at his lover. "And I think Marybeth might have gutted you if you made her into a deformed house cat. Do you make each member one in their own likeness now?"

Levi looked relieved as he came closer. "I'm working on it. This one kind of started it." He ran a finger down the wooden leopard's nose. "Grandma Marybeth wanted one after she saw it, then Mom wanted one, and Drake and Jenny—maybe we're a vain lot of leopards," he said then chuckled as if he were embarrassed at the possibility.

"Nah." Lyndon wouldn't mind having one of himself in cougar form to sit across from Levi's.

"I could make you one," Levi offered.

Lyndon pulled his hand back and tipped his head to the side to look at Levi. "How the hell do you know what I'm thinking?"

Levi blinked then rubbed at his forehead. "I don't know. I'm sorry if it bugs you. I don't try to, I just, I get these impressions. It's not consistent and it's probably invasive anyway, but I don't do it on purpose."

Lyndon considered it and shrugged. It had to be weird for Levi. "Ever done it to anyone else?"

"No," Levi answered immediately. "I don't want to, either. I can't imagine picking up on other people's emotions or whatever. I'd never leave the cabin again. Or at least I wouldn't go around other people, I guess. Does it—does it bother you?"

He looked so distressed Lyndon couldn't keep from pulling him in for a hug. "No, it doesn't. Not like I have anything to hide. I can't do it to you, but I realised earlier I can read you probably just as effectively. You have a very expressive face, and your eyes, well, they give everything away." At least for him they did.

"Makes it kind of fair then, isn't it?"

"It is," Lyndon agreed. "Now, let's get the spunk and blood washed off and see if we can—"

"Ah, damn it!" Levi groaned. "Hurry up, hurry! My parents are on their way, and they'll barge right in!"

"How—" Lyndon started to ask as Levi dragged him down the hall.

"I guess my senses are really sharper than yours, at least when we're human." He opened a door and pushed Lyndon into the bathroom. "Quick, turn the water on, I have to run back for our clothes!"

Lyndon didn't need his shifter senses to hear the front door open then slam followed by two voices calling out for Levi. He could even hear them over the shower running.

"Shit shit shit!" Levi looked as panicked as he sounded. "Get in," he gritted out. "Showering, be out in a few minutes," he bellowed towards the door.

"Did you lock it?" Lyndon asked.

"Fuck. No." Levi did so then while Lyndon got in the shower. It was nice sized, dual showerheads. Too bad they weren't going to get to really enjoy those this time around.

"Levi, I expect you and your *friend* out in ten minutes!" The deep, masculine voice sounded almost as sexy as Levi's, yet Lyndon couldn't quite stop a little shiver from racing down his back.

"Your father, I take it?"

Levi's cheeks were flaming and his mouth was pinched into a thin line. "Yeah. You'd think I was thirteen not twenty-three."

"I heard that," the man boomed through the door. "And I don't care how old you are, you're always going to be our son! Now hurry up!"

"No wonder I've never brought anyone home."

Levi might have meant to tease, but Lyndon couldn't stop the growl those words caused. "That's not why, is it, Levi?" he asked. He took Levi's cock in hand and squeezed.

Levi shivered despite the warm temperature of the water. His cock filled and Lyndon pumped it mercilessly. "Is it?" Lyndon prodded again.

"No, it's not," Levi stuttered, bracing himself on the wall by leaning back until his shoulders pressed to the blue tiles. "Oh fuck, Lyndon, keep doing on and I'm gonna—"

"I know," Lyndon said with a feral twist of his lips. "You're going to come, which is exactly what I intend to happen."

Levi wasn't a child, and his parents' concern was all well and good, but this was Levi's house, and he was Levi's lover, and Lyndon wasn't going to let this quick shower be a total waste. And he doubted Levi would be able to be quiet.

"God, Lyndon, please," Levi rasped, and Lyndon rewarded him by catching his nail in Levi's slit. "Ah!" Levi's eyes shot wide open and he slapped a hand over his mouth. "Mmmph!" Levi grunted through his climax.

Lyndon dropped to his knees and sucked the last spurt down, holding Levi's legs wide open by gripping the insides of his strong thighs. Lyndon lapped the tip of Levi's cock then licked down the underside. He buried his face in Levi's balls, drawing the scent there deep into his lungs. Levi whimpered and Lyndon hummed, pressing his lips to Levi's nuts for a quick kiss before standing.

He rubbed against Levi and peered into his slumberous eyes. "When they leave…" That was all he had to say.

Levi was nodding his head eagerly. "Whatever you want, when they leave."

What Lyndon wanted was to be alone with Levi for several hours, long enough for him to taste every inch of his skin and learn all the contours of Levi's body, the curves of muscle and the hard ridges too. He wanted to know what drove Levi crazy with passion, what he couldn't stand so Lyndon would never cross a line he shouldn't.

Instead he was fixing to meet Levi's parents, and frankly, he was scared. Nervous sounded better, but so much rested on Levi's family accepting him. Oh, not right away, certainly, but if they hated him right off the bat and wanted him gone, what then? He'd talked big to Marybeth, saying it was up to Levi whether or not he stayed here—and that was the truth—but what if Levi's parents wanted him gone? Would Levi cave in to family pressure? Lyndon feared he would. After all, Levi loved his family, and they obviously loved him.

Lyndon was, for all anyone knew, just a flash in the pan, a quick fuck Levi might easily tire of. Except, Lyndon didn't believe any such thing. Levi wouldn't have brought him here, into this very personal space, wouldn't have exposed his family to Lyndon, if Levi hadn't already had some strong feelings for him. And maybe those feelings were just lust, but Lyndon had to think something more could grow from them.

Something stronger, more enduring. Hopefully, Levi's family would believe it, too.

"Don't be nervous." Levi caressed Lyndon's shoulder. "They're going to like you, just as Grandma does. She wouldn't have left me alone with you otherwise."

It unnerved Lyndon a little, the way Levi picked up on what he was thinking so easily—but not it didn't unnerve him as much as it should, a fact he was aware of. Yet he liked having such a close bond with Levi already. It felt...good, safe. Right.

"I just don't want to blow it, you know," Lyndon confessed. "I mean, I know you love them, and I don't want you to be in an awkward position."

Levi leered at him and turned off the water. "Oh, but I like awkward positions! Or at least, I think I'll like them. There's a few—"

Lyndon laughed and popped Levi on the butt just because they'd both enjoy it. "All right, all right, let's get out there and do this before I lose my nerve."

"You won't lose your nerve," Levi said with a certainty Lyndon wished he could feel. And maybe he could, if he started to believe in himself again. Lyndon thought he could do it, for himself, and for Levi.

"We'd better hurry and get out there." Levi tossed a towel at Lyndon. "I wouldn't put it past my dad to just pick the lock or something. When he said ten minutes, he meant it, I'm sure."

Lyndon would have liked more time, and he really wished he had an idea of what to expect with this meeting. Although, maybe he did. He knew Levi was a good man, respectful of his elders and loving his family. He had most likely been taught those qualities, or encouraged to express them, whatever parenting term was correct for raising up a good kid. Anyway, he had to have learned those things from his parents, Lyndon figured. Which meant, he hoped, they'd be just incredible as Levi, and even Marybeth.

He told himself over and over to relax, but he was still a bundle of nerves when he stepped out of the bathroom.

# Chapter Thirteen

Levi loved his parents—all of his family, for that matter—but sometimes he wished he lived far, far away from them. Like when he was still a puddle of gelatinous goo on the inside from Lyndon's touch. He just wanted to snuggle up in bed with his lover and revel in the warm buzz of happiness being near Lyndon gave him.

Instead he was going to be hanging with the parents and introducing them to his—well, to Lyndon. Levi wasn't a hundred percent clear just what Lyndon was to him. Hell, he wasn't even fifty percent clear on the terminology he should use when describing their budding relationship. But he was positive what was building between him and Lyndon was something very unique and strong.

He finished getting his clothes on and planted a noisy kiss on Lyndon's cheek as soon as his head appeared through the T-shirt opening. "Come on, let me show you how amazing my family is." Another kiss, this one to Lyndon's lips, and both of them were a tad breathless when they left the bathroom.

Levi's dad stood at the entry of the hallway, hovering like some worried mama bear. Levi kept one of Lyndon's hands in his as they stopped in front of Henry. "Dad, this is Lyndon Hines. Lyndon, my dad, Henry Travis."

"Good to meet you," Lyndon said, returning Henry's intense look. "You have an incredible son."

"We do," Levi's mom said coming in from the kitchen. "In fact, all of our kids are pretty incredible. Sometimes even in a good way."

Henry laughed and Levi groaned at the bad joke, but Lyndon seemed unsure of what his reaction was supposed to be. Levi mouthed "Just be yourself" before reaching out to give his mom a one-armed hug. "Tell me you and Dad aren't staying long," he whispered near her ear.

Cheryl chuckled. "Sure." She nudged him away and looked Lyndon up and down. "Well, I can see why Levi might be fascinated with you. I'm Cheryl, and you'd better be good to my boy."

"Yes ma'am." Lyndon smiled and shook Cheryl's hand. He didn't offer a cheesy compliment to Cheryl, for which Levi was grateful. His mother hated bullshit. "Am I going to be interrogated?"

"I think he's got us figured out," Henry said after laughing and slapping Lyndon on the back. "And yes, probably at least a little."

"Right. We'll try not to be too obnoxious about it, but..." Cheryl let loose a long sigh. "Well, Levi, you remember how we all, er, chatted with Jenny's Mark when she brought him over the first time."

*Oh shit!* "Uh, yeah." Poor Mark had looked like he wanted to run. Jenny hadn't let go of his hand the whole two hours he'd been over. And Levi had been there, too.

Which Cheryl, of course, pointed out. "I thought you were going to take Mark out back for a man to man talk." The way she said it left no doubt as to how the talking would have played out—with fists. Which wasn't true. Mostly.

"I didn't say anything about fighting Mark and you know it," Levi groused, barely holding on to his temper. Lyndon didn't need to be teased when he'd been so nervous in the first place. "And I only did what Dad told me to do, which was look intimidating."

"Don't blame it on me, you were eager enough to go along."

"Both of you about scared that poor boy—young man," Cheryl corrected quickly, "to death. We aren't going to let anyone try it with you, Lyndon."

Lyndon didn't look convinced. "And why am I an exception?"

Henry sat down in the big recliner. "You're not, we just couldn't figure out who we could get to intimidate you. You're kinda big."

Levi tugged and got Lyndon settled on the couch with him. Lyndon was just the right size, in his opinion, but he wasn't going to comment unless his parents had some other devious plan up their sleeves. Like to pull out a chart and start ticking off plus and minuses in regards to Lyndon's suitability. *This is what comes from having a close family.* He patted Lyndon's leg reassuringly, he hoped.

"Besides, Jenny was really angry with us after the whole...interrogation. We realised we were probably overprotective since she was our first child to fall in love." Cheryl sat down on the arm of Henry's chair. "Now, we aren't saying you two are in love, but Levi hasn't ever brought a boyfriend home before, and we've never met any other shifters, so we're doubly curious."

"About?" Lyndon sounded so calm Levi had to look hard to detect the tense set to his jaw and the small tic there by the join. Levi wanted to smooth away the tension and the twitch, but wasn't willing to give away the signs of Lyndon's discomfort to his parent. Lyndon had his emotions reined in tight, not even giving off a whiff of a nervous air. Levi was happy to let him have the comfort of such self-control.

"Well, about you personally, of course, but also about what you are." Cheryl's smiled ruefully. "We didn't know there were other types of shifters. Kind of egotistical of us to think snow leopards were the only kind, I suppose. Honestly, though, I never gave it much thought. I've been too busy loving and enjoying my life—but that doesn't mean I don't want to know about our past."

Lyndon relaxed fractionally and draped his arm over Levi's shoulders. "I don't know a whole lot about shifters, Cheryl. My mother wasn't one, and I don't know my father."

Cheryl leant forward and for a second Levi thought she was going to get up and come and hug Lyndon. He wasn't sure if he should be relieved she didn't. "You don't know him? Like, who he is, or just aren't close to him?"

"Prying a lot, aren't you?" Levi interjected. "I thought this wasn't going to be another interrogation."

"It's okay. I understand why they want to know these things." Lyndon smiled at him and Levi knew he was telling the truth. "I like that your family loves you enough to be intrusive and"—Lyndon winked at Cheryl—"Borderline rude."

## Levi

"Borderline, my butt," Levi grumbled. He couldn't tell who laughed louder, his mom or dad. "This is an example of the love hurts theory. Or at least, love embarrasses."

Lyndon nuzzled Levi's cheek, then his ear. "Be glad you have them, Levi."

"Oh, I do like him, son." Cheryl hummed a little and settled back against Henry's arm behind her. "He might even be a keeper."

Levi wanted to call her on the 'might' part, but he saw the way her eyes held a teasing glint and he let it go. Instead, he returned his attention to Lyndon. "Do you want me to run them off?"

Lyndon took a few seconds to answer, but he sounded certain once he did. "No, I think maybe I need to talk about my father and why I've been running for so long."

# Chapter Fourteen

Whether it was a need to belong, or simply being able to actually talk freely about his past, Lyndon couldn't say, but he found himself opening up. The words almost gushed from him, as if they'd been held back so long the pressure of keeping them inside had grown too great to be restricted any longer.

Lyndon began speaking, his gaze darting from Cheryl to Henry then to Levi and back again. "My father is, it turns out, a very wealthy man. Also very territorial, and when I did meet him, it wasn't what you'd call a friendly confrontation. He attacked me when I was a scared kid whose mom had just died. And he drove me from the only familiar place I had."

Cheryl's normally fair skin had gone even paler, and Henry had pulled her down onto his lap as Lyndon had spoken. Her voice held a slight quaver when she spoke. "What kind of father would do something so awful? How old were you?"

"A cruel one, and I was seventeen, almost an adult." Lyndon settled a little closer to Levi. "My mom had struggled with bipolar disorder for as long as I could remember. She'd been disowned by her family because of it, she told me once. Her highs were...were dangerous times, for her and sometimes for me, but she wasn't a bad person. She wasn't a bad mother. She was just ill, and there was no one or way for her to get the help she needed."

Levi could tell Cheryl wanted to ask how Lyndon's mother had died, but good manners held her back. "First of all, you weren't an adult, period. Age doesn't make one an adult, either, not in my opinion. I can't imagine..." Cheryl's voice cracked and she cleared her throat. "I'm sorry you had to go through losing your mother alone. It's horrible that her family held a disease she couldn't control against her. How did you get along after she passed away?"

"The day I found her..." Lyndon gulped and turned his gaze towards his hand in Levi's. "Everything about it is blurry, which is probably for the best. I got up to go to school, and went to check on her. She was just...it was like she was asleep, except her eyes—" It hurt to remember, which was more than likely the reason he didn't remember much of that horrible day. "The official cause of death was listed as natural causes. I've never figured out what the meant, when a thirty-six year old woman goes to sleep and never wakes up. Doesn't seem natural to me."

"Lyndon."

He forced himself to look at Levi and told himself there was no shame in the way his eyes burned with unshed tears. Levi cupped Lyndon's nape and pulled his head close until their foreheads touched. "You don't have to keep talking. I hate seeing you hurting."

Lyndon rocked his brow on Levi's, small movements, but comforting ones. "I've never really gotten to talk about any of this before, Levi. It...it helps even if it hurts." In fact, the more he spoke, the lighter he seemed to feel even though he ached. He was finally mourning in a way he hadn't been able to before. Another band of emotional steel loosened inside.

"An anonymous donor paid for a very basic funeral." Lyndon sighed and reached over his lap to take Levi's hand. "I suspect it was my father, Cole Tavares, who paid for it. There was only me and our neighbour along with some people I didn't recognise at the funeral. Turned out one of those was my father."

"He actually had the nerve to show up then?" Henry growled, sounding very much like a shifter even though he wasn't.

Lyndon nodded. "Yeah. He pulled me aside afterwards, took me back to the only home I'd known for years, then proceeded to beat the shit out of me. Then he told me he held the lien on our home, and gave me a cheque before driving me out of San Antonio and tossing me out in an area where a few gang victims' bodies had been found over the years. I remember hitting the ground, then I came to with an old, grizzled guy leaning over me. His name was Grady Marks, and he's the reason I'm still alive today. I think I'd have just given up without him."

Cheryl stood up and walked over before sitting beside him. She touched his arm but didn't push for anything more affectionate, which was good with Lyndon since he didn't know her or Henry at all, really.

"I think you'd have still been here," Cheryl said. "You might have had a bumpier road, but you'd have stayed on it. You're a strong young man, Lyndon. I wouldn't expect Levi to fall for anyone who wasn't."

Was that the parental blessing couples were always hoping for? Lyndon kind of thought it was. And Cheryl was giving him a look he didn't quite know how to interpret, but it was—it reminded him of the way his mom would look at him, all soft and caring, and he'd missed that, so very, very much.

He leaned over and kissed Cheryl's cheek, hoping he wasn't reading too much into her expression. "Thank you."

Cheryl squeezed his arm. "Any time you need to talk, Lyndon, we're here." She stood up after patting him. "Now, we're getting dangerously close to being nice." Cheryl winked at him. "Wouldn't want to ruin our reputations as the big, bad interrogators."

"Too late," Levi crooned. "You and Dad have already exposed your inner gooey sweetness, and now Lyndon's going to know what big softies you both are. If you aren't nice to him, he'll warn all the other boyfriends or girlfriends the sibs bring around later on."

From there on, the conversations were much more light-hearted. Lyndon was relieved in a way, but he also thought he'd like to talk to Levi about his past sometime, maybe once they had spent more time together.

He also enjoyed watching the way Cheryl and Henry were with each other. Their love was as obvious as their respect for one another. Lyndon had wondered about it, since Cheryl was a shifter and Henry wasn't, there'd be some sort of power imbalance, like where Cheryl was more the boss and Henry the obedient worker, but it seemed they had a true partnership, equal and loving. Lyndon wanted that for himself, and he wanted it for and with Levi.

Tonight, he thought it just might be possible to have it, given time.

"I really think I'm going to like your parents," he told Levi after Cheryl and Henry left.

Levi made an exasperated sound and flopped on the couch. "You already like them, and I'd love them even more if they didn't stay so long!"

Lyndon laughed and reached for Levi. "You couldn't possibly love them any more than you already do. You know how great they are."

Levi came up and into his arms in a fluid motion. "You're right. Now, why don't you take me to bed and show me how great you are."

"Sounds like the best suggestion I've heard all evening."

# Chapter Fifteen

The warm body sprawled over his was a delight to wake up to. Levi opened his eyes, eager to see Lyndon. That Lyndon hadn't packed up and left after being grilled by Levi's parents was kind of miraculous. Once Lyndon had told them, and Levi, about his past, Levi's parents had all but pronounced Lyndon their son-in-law. Embarrassing, kind of, but also just...cool.

Levi took a minute to enjoy the way Lyndon's weight felt on him. Levi was lying on his back, and Lyndon had an arm and a leg over him. He was also lying somewhat on his stomach and somewhat on Levi. The hard press of Lyndon's dick to his hip was definitely promising. Levi cautiously stroked a hand down Lyndon's back, his feather-light touch bringing goose bumps to Lyndon's skin. Levi couldn't imagine not having his parents around. Having his father run him off, his mother die—just, no. It made his heart ache to think of what Lyndon must have felt. If he had his way, Lyndon would never feel unwanted again.

And now with Levi's family on Lyndon's side—if all of them weren't yet, they would be, Grandma Marybeth would see to it—maybe they could figure out who was hunting Lyndon, and why. Levi agreed with Lyndon that whoever it was seemed to be getting a kick out of playing with him, but Levi was glad that was all it had been so far. Otherwise, the night in Pennsylvania Lyndon had told him about... Levi shuddered and clasped Lyndon's hip. He wouldn't think about what could have happened then, either.

"Wha—" Lyndon grumbled and opened one eye. The sun streaming through the window made the iris look burnished gold-flecked spots and darker hints of amber. That eye crinkled at the outer corner and Lyndon bumped his cock against Levi's hip. "Morning."

"Yeah, it is," Levi said, sure he sounded smug uttering even those three words. His ass was sore, his neck stiff and a few places on his body felt hot where the scratches Lyndon had left on him tingled. Lust brought Levi's dick to full attention. Considering they had rubbed off on each other during the night, a slow, gentle mating the polar opposite of the first one they'd shared in the woods, then Lyndon had proceeded to suck Levi's brains out of his dick a couple of hours later. Levi was kind of surprised he could even get it up again. But up, it was.

Levi nudged Lyndon over onto his back, grinning at the way the man's thick cock slapped his belly. Levi knew what that monster felt like splitting his ass, what it felt like in his hand and rutting on him, but what he didn't know and was going to find out was how it felt against his tongue.

"Gonna make it a very good morning, too," Levi murmured as he began kissing Lyndon's neck.

"Yeah, let's do that." Lyndon's hands were in his hair, his fingers tightening as he pushed at Levi's head.

Levi nipped the warm skin beneath which he could feel Lyndon's pulse. Then he sealed his lips around it and sucked as Lyndon's breath hitched and those hands stopped pushing and started pressing. Levi would have chuckled if his mouth hadn't been otherwise occupied.

Lyndon slipped one hand down Levi's neck until he touched the bite mark. There he rubbed, and it was Levi's turn to lose his breath.

"You like that, don't you?"

As if Lyndon needed to ask. Levi scooted to where he could get some contact with Lyndon's leg. He desperately craved friction for his dick.

"Why don't you bring your morning wood up here instead of rubbing off on my leg," Lyndon suggested.

Levi lifted his head enough to say, "'Kay," then he did a one-eighty in record time.

Lyndon grabbed his hips and pulled. "Bring your ass down here. Can't think of a better thing to eat for breakfast."

Like he was going to argue about *that*. Levi had been rimmed exactly once before, another experience with Yancy and it hadn't been a good one, either. Hearing 'yuck' and '*why* do people do this? I don't care if it's clean, there could still be germs' was just a total turn off. Levi was so eager he bumped Lyndon's nose.

"Careful," Lyndon said, sounding amused. "Ease back."

Levi did and was rewarded by a rough lick over his hole. "Oh God, how'm I supposed to blow you when you do that?"

A puff of warm air over his hole then another lick and Levi dropped to his elbows and whimpered. Lyndon's cock was right there, large and dripping, and no matter what was happening to his ass, Levi couldn't ignore that shaft.

Levi lifted it from the base then laid a wet stripe over the head. Lyndon's salty tang hit his tongue at the same time Lyndon's speared into Levi's pucker. Their gasps were almost simultaneous. Levi parted his lips and sucked the fat crown into his mouth.as Lyndon pried his ass cheeks further apart and started seriously going to town on Levi's hole.

Levi loosened his jaw and slurped down Lyndon's cock, making it a noisy, messy slide. He wanted Lyndon to hear as well as feel what Levi was doing to him. Levi took Lyndon's length into his throat and swallowed then he cupped Lyndon's furry balls.

Lyndon's reaction was instantaneous. He bucked and buried his dick a fraction deeper, making breathing a tricky thing. It excited Levi almost as much as the scrape of teeth over his tender hole. When he rocked back for more of Lyndon's mouth, he slid his up Lyndon's dick, sucking hard and dragging a moan from Lyndon that vibrated against Levi's opening. Levi flicked his tongue over Lyndon's frenulum then let his teeth catch the rim of the crown. Lyndon slammed his hips up and jerked Levi's ass down before plunging what had to be at least a couple of fingers into Levi's hole.

Levi sputtered, his mouth and ass stuffed, then he began moving, finding a rhythm that brought him almost off Lyndon's fingers when he deep-throated his cock. Then Levi sucked on just the spongy glans and shoved his ass back to bury Lyndon's fingers deep.

Lyndon squeezed and slapped Levi's cheeks which made him desperate to come. Levi whimpered around the dick in his mouth and set about driving Lyndon insane. Licking, sucking, using his teeth and fingers, rolling and tugging on Lyndon's balls, Levi used everything he had. When he pressed his fingers to the silky skin beneath Lyndon's sac, he jerked so hard he nearly tossed Levi off.

But Lyndon held onto to him, keeping an arm around Levi's hips, then his hot mouth sealed over Levi's balls and his fingers shoved deep, the increased intensity of the stretch telling Levi there was a hell of a lot more fingers than two in his ass. He sucked hard and massaged Lyndon's prostate from the outside while Lyndon massaged his internally. Levi shook and pumped his hips, undulated and moaned and finally keened when Lyndon nipped the crown of his dick.

Levi came so hard it hurt, the first shot barrelling up his cock and shooting out with enough force the splat of impact sounded in Levi's ears. Afterwards, he didn't hear much beside his own mewls as he emptied his balls onto Lyndon.

Once Levi could breathe, think, he sat up and scooted around until he could aim Lyndon's cock at his hole.

Lyndon wiggled beneath him then tapped Levi's hip with a condom. "Put it on me."

Levi took the lubed rubber and slowly rolled it over Lyndon's shaft, regretting he wouldn't be feeling Lyndon's cum warming his insides. Maybe, if they were tested—but Levi wasn't sure how or if testing could happen. The last thing any of them needed was to be busted having altered DNA. Pushing aside the problem of how to get tested for now, Levi rubbed Lyndon's dick against his butt.

"Yeah, ride me just like that," Lyndon urged, settling his hands on Levi's hips.

"Going to, gonna blow your mind." Levi held Lyndon's dick at the root and slowly sank down on it. The burn was wonderful, the added bit of pain Levi loved making his dick twitch. Levi glanced at his shaft. *Not happening, buddy.* He rocked back and moved his hand out of the way as he filled his ass, taking Lyndon's cock as quickly as he could. "Ahhh..." Levi dropped his chin to his chest and placed his hands on the mattress and began to ride Lyndon, desperate to hear his shout when he climaxed.

Lyndon's nails brought heat to Levi's hips, digging into his skin. Levi turned his head enough to see the black-tipped nails piercing him. He brought his hand up to pinch his nipple, and Lyndon sat up. In a flash, Levi was on his belly, his arm pinned beneath him as Lyndon growled and shoved his cock back into Levi's hole.

"Fuck yes," Levi hissed, wishing he could come again. Lyndon was fucking him so hard, so deep, so perfect Levi could do nothing but try to arch into each thrust.

"Gonna make you come again," Lyndon snarled against his ear. He topped the promise off with a bite to the shell of Levi's ear. Then Lyndon braced himself on Levi's shoulders, and Levi discovered what it meant to really have his ass ploughed.

He grunted every time Lyndon penetrated him, whined and pleaded each time he withdrew. His cock hardened, ached as Lyndon pounded into him. Levi's breaths were short, shallow, Lyndon's weight keeping him from inhaling deeply. Lyndon cursed and rose to his knees, looping an arm under Levi to pull him up as well.

Lyndon wrapped his other arm around Levi's chest, scratching his way to Levi's throat. He closed his hand over the front of it, not quite squeezing, but the thought that he could, that Lyndon might choose to cut off his breath was more stimulation, darkly arousing, and Levi had to grab his dick, only a little surprised to find it hard.

"Do it," Lyndon ordered, and he pressed his palm ti Levi's neck. "Now!"

He thrust and filled Levi so full, so perfectly, he didn't ever want Lyndon to stop.

Levi spread the pre-cum on his crown down as much as he could. Lyndon fucked him so hard Levi's hand slipped on his tip and he knew they'd both be bruised come tomorrow if not sooner. Lyndon leant a hand, closing it around his, helping to capture Levi's dick in a steely, vice-like grip. Levi let Lyndon set the pace, rough, fast, the same as the way Lyndon was drilling his ass.

Then Lyndon pulled Levi's neck to the side and bit the tender spot where shoulder and neck join.

Levi screamed, pain morphing into pleasure too intense to bear. His cock pulsed and cum spurted out.

"Fuck yeah," Lyndon rasped against Levi's neck then he cursed again and jammed his cock in once, twice.

Heat flooded Levi's ass through the condom, Lyndon's spunk warming him inside as his own cum splattered his hand.

"Oh my God," Levi muttered once he stopped shaking. "You're gonna kill me. Death by climax."

"You and me both," Lyndon replied. "I thought one was going to stop my heart. Come here." He eased back, taking Levi with him.

Levi whimpered when Lyndon's cock slipped free.

After a few minutes to gather their wits, Levi rolled onto his side and looked at Lyndon. His eyes were open, his lips tipped up in a heart-warming smile. Lyndon tucked a chunk of hair behind Levi's ear. It was a tender gesture, one which reassured Levi there was more to them, would be more to them, than fucking. Not that he didn't love that part, though, but he did want them to enjoy many other things together as well.

"What's the plan for the day?" Lyndon asked.

Levi thought about the order he had to finish. "Got a chair to do, but we should probably shower and eat something first."

Lyndon nodded. "Yup. Bet there will be more of your family coming by, too. I haven't met your brothers Drake, and Orion. Oscar will probably be by to threaten to have me stuffed at least once."

Levi snorted. "Yeah. You're lucky my sister Jenny and her husband Mark live in Colorado Springs. Though they might just show up this weekend."

"Probably. You've got a nice family," Lyndon said gruffly.

Levi smiled and dropped a kiss on Lyndon's lips. "I do, and I'll share them, if you'd like."

The smile those words brought to Lyndon's mouth was worth everything Levi had.

# Chapter Sixteen

Lyndon wasn't too far off about Oscar. The man showed up banging on the bedroom door and startling Lyndon and Levi out of a sound sleep. Levi yelped and clipped Lyndon's nose with his elbow.

"Ow," Lyndon grumbled, pinching his nose. His eyes watered as Oscar added hollering to his morning wake-up call.

"Get up! You have to finish the Aberdeen's order!"

"Jerk," Levi muttered. He rolled to his side and gasped. "Shit! Are you okay? I'm sorry! I didn't mean to hit you!"

Lyndon caught Levi's hand before he could poke at Lyndon's nose. "It's fine. Just make him shut up already."

"I'm going to open the door at the count of five," Oscar warned.

Levi was up off the bed like he'd been catapulted. "You don't have a key, and we are up thanks to all of the racket you're making!"

"I don't need a key, I can pick the lock."

"Fuck off," Levi mumbled as he grabbed a pair of jeans from the closet.

"I heard you, Levi," Oscar called through the door. "Just for that, I'm only going to fix breakfast for your boyfriend."

"I'd be scared to eat it considering the threats you've made." Lyndon made sure he said it loud enough, Oscar would have no doubt he'd meant to be heard.

There was a moment of silence then, "You're smarter than I thought," Oscar said. "But Grandma Marybeth would skin me, and since you didn't maim my brother or abandon him again, I might reconsider the whole taxidermy thing."

Lyndon still wasn't sure Oscar had ever been joking about the taxidermy to begin with. He was inclined to believe Oscar hadn't been, so he'd take whatever he could get in the way of a peace offering. He heard Oscar's thudding footsteps and got out of the bed. His clothes from yesterday were all he had that his stalker hadn't marked so he started to pick his jeans up only to be stopped when Levi handed him a bundle of clothes.

"Here, I have sweats and a shirt. Socks and underwear are in the top drawer." Levi pulled a ratty-looking green shirt on over his head then arched a brow at Lyndon. "I better get in the kitchen before Oscar does try to cook. Last time he caught my stove top on fire."

Lyndon arched an eyebrow right back. "Wait! You can't leave now without explaining how Oscar set your stove on fire!"

"Let me just say, while my brother is brilliant, he didn't know you should smother a grease fire instead of dumping water on it." Then Levi was out the door

## Levi

and, from the sound of it, running towards the kitchen.

Lyndon would have chuckled over Oscar's mistake if he hadn't done the same thing himself. Of course, he'd been an eleven-year-old kid trying to fix dinner in the hopes of getting his mom to eat.

"Don't go there." Those were memories Lyndon didn't want to get lost in right now. He walked to the dresser and found the rest of the clothing he needed.

After he finished using the toilet, Lyndon started to turn on the sink when he heard a knock on the front door. He recognised the voices of Henry and Cheryl, Levi and Oscar's parents, but the other two male voices weren't familiar. Lyndon couldn't quite make out what was being said, but there was something about the low tones that made his skin itch. He grabbed the toothpaste and, unable to find an extra toothbrush, used Levi's to get rid of his funky morning breath. Lyndon dressed quickly, glad the sweats and shirt were only a little snug. Levi wasn't much smaller than him at all.

Lyndon splashed his face a couple of times and gave the shower a wistful look before trying to de-fluff his hair. At least it wasn't all over the place like it used to be when he'd lived in Dallas. The humidity had never failed to make his hair frizzy to the extreme. There just weren't enough styling products in the world to combat Texas humidity.

Satisfied he looked as presentable as possible, Lyndon sucked in a deep breath and told himself to man up. He couldn't help but feel a little intimidated by Levi's family. Not that he thought they were going to run him off—he hoped they wouldn't—but he hadn't had a lot of experience interacting with family. There'd only been his mother, and she'd been lost in her own world much of the time those last few years. Then he'd met his dad —

*Stop stalling.*

Laughter rang out from the kitchen as Lyndon stepped into the hall. He hesitated, uncomfortable for a moment and not wanting to intrude. It shouldn't have surprised him at all that Levi appeared in the kitchen doorway almost immediately. The soft smile the man wore matched the soft glow in his green eyes. Lyndon stopped worrying about how and if he would fit in when Levi held out his hand.

"It'll be fine," Levi said so quietly Lyndon had to strain to hear, but he bet Levi's family heard with those sharp senses they retained in human form. "Come meet the rest of the crew. Well, not all the rest of them, but my two other brothers. I imagine you'll be meeting Jenny and Mark soon enough."

It was nice, Levi's hand in his. Lyndon had never been big on public displays of affection, but they weren't in public and even if they had been, he'd have wanted the intimacy of the simple touch.

"Took you long enough," Oscar said, grabbing a slice of bacon off a platter on the table.

Henry lightly tapped the back of Oscar's head as he smiled at Lyndon. "Ignore him, and be glad we brought breakfast over. Levi can cook, but he doesn't have my recipe for buttermilk biscuits."

The red ceramic bowl Henry took out of the oven was full of steaming hot biscuits, and the scent wafting off them was drool-worthy. Lyndon's mouth watered as Henry set the biscuits on the table. Cheryl came in through the back door followed by two stoic-looking young men. Cheryl seemed...worried? Lyndon must not have been the only one who thought so because Henry and Oscar descended on her.

## Levi

"What's wrong?" Henry asked, glancing from Cheryl to each of the men behind him.

Cheryl peered past Henry at Lyndon, and Lyndon didn't need any extra senses to tell him what she was going to say next. It still hit him like a punch to the diaphragm. "There's cougar tracks outside, among other...evidence...of another cat being here."

Lyndon said the first thing that came to his mind, even if it was what he wanted least—for himself, anyway. "I should leave." He wanted Levi and his family safe.

"Fuck that," Levi snapped, locking an arm around Lyndon's waist.

"What he said," Oscar muttered, glaring at the back door as if he could visually exterminate Lyndon's stalker.

"Watch your mouth, Levi Allen! And you, Lyndon, you're not going anywhere." Henry turned to face Lyndon fully "You know you're welcome here, wanted, even. Don't you think you've found something worth fighting for? Some*one*?"

Lyndon looked at him, at the rest of the family who were watching him intently in return. Levi's gaze drew his and Lyndon nodded. "More than just someone." He swallowed around a tight knot of emotion threatening to clog his throat. "There's a whole family here worth fighting for." Maybe they weren't his family, not yet, but Lyndon wanted them to be. He wanted to be a part of this group of people who loved and protected each other.

Levi's smile was so sweet it made Lyndon's heart quiver as warmth spread to his fingertips. "Then let's sit down and figure out a plan to end this shit."

"Language, Levi," Cheryl scolded. He got popped just like Oscar had earlier.

"Ow," Levi grumbled as he rubbed his head.

"And we will have a nice, enjoyable family breakfast before we start dealing with anything else. would have joined us but she'd already made plans with Betta."

"Betta's Cheryl's sister," Henry explained, "and Marybeth's youngest daughter. She lives in Colorado Springs."

Lyndon nodded and decided he might just have to draw out a family tree. He knew Marybeth and her deceased husband Vincent had several kids and keeping track of *their* kids and so on was going to be a challenge.

Cheryl turned and gestured towards the table. "Drake, Orion, help your mother get the rest of the food on the table."

The two men behind Henry scuttled to the stove and began carrying plates loaded with pancakes and sausage as well as a big bowl of creamy white gravy.

"Drake's the one who looks the most like me," Levi said as he nudged Lyndon towards the table. "Obviously Orion resembles us too, though."

"Hey." Orion waved at Lyndon.

Drake just tipped his chin then started rearranging the platters to some pattern only he could comprehend.

Lyndon thought the description of both brothers apt. Drake could have been Levi's twin if Levi had been a couple of inches shorter and his hair a shade lighter and streaked with burgundy chunks. Orion had hair that wasn't black, but it was so dark a brown it probably appeared so in weaker lighting. He also had harsher features, as if he'd got an extra dose of testosterone in the womb or something. As far as appearances went, he looked like the toughest of the brothers.

Henry started handing out orders as he brought honey, butter and jam to the table. "Levi, Lyndon, can you get the silverware and plates? And Oscar, get the glasses. Your mom will get the milk and OJ."

"Almost got us seated," Levi said, obviously thinking he was safe from another swat since his mother's hands were full.

"She's gonna sit that stuff down in just a second," Lyndon warned.

Henry and Drake laughed while Oscar and Orion nodded.

"Yes, you know she will just wait to get you when you're not expecting it," Henry pointed out. "You're going to be sitting there, minding your own business, and this petite blonde angel is going to sneak up and smack you into next week."

"Angel my butt," Cheryl snorted, "but the rest of it was pretty accurate."

The teasing banter helped lift a little of the stress off Lyndon's shoulders and he found himself able to relax to an extent and enjoy the meal. Levi's brothers were something else. Actually, all of Cheryl and Henry's sons were something else. Levi picked and teased as much if not more than the other three young men. It was amusing to watch and made for one of the most pleasant—or maybe humorous was more apt—meals Lyndon had ever had.

But the meal eventually ended, and the joking camaraderie died down as Cheryl cleared her throat. Lyndon fought the urge to fold his hands in his lap like a scared kid. He wasn't scared, not for himself anyway. As for Levi and his family, Lyndon would fight to the death to protect them.

"It won't come to that," Levi told him, placing his hand on top of Lyndon's.

Lyndon turned his hand palm up, slipping his fingers between Levi's while he lost himself his man's eyes for a second or two.

"Won't let what come to what?" Drake asked in a voice almost as deep as Levi's.

Levi saved Lyndon from trying to come up with an explanation. "I was just thinking out loud, never mind me."

Drake didn't look entirely convinced. "Is there something going on? I mean, between you two that the family should know about—besides the obvious," Drake tacked on when Levi started to chuckle. Drake scowled but his sparkling eyes gave away his amusement. "Seriously, Grandma Marybeth doesn't remember much. We don't really know a lot about what we are, so if there's some new development—"

"Can't you smell their connection?" Orion looked straight at Lyndon, pinning him with a dark, unwavering gaze. "It's like the established relationships, like Mom and Dad, and they've only just hooked up. Is this a cougar thing?"

Lyndon was uncomfortably aware of everyone looking at him now, expecting a confirmation he just couldn't give. Grady had spent more time teaching Lyndon to be a decent human being than dwelling on their shifter natures. "I don't know for sure, but I don't think so," he admitted. "I mean, my father didn't seem to give a shit about my mom, and as far as I know he never married."

Levi squeezed his hand and Lyndon tilted towards him a little, grateful for the comfort Levi offered.

"Maybe he just never met the right person. For all we know, he could fall in love tomorrow and maybe not be such a total...jerk."

Lyndon wished he could believe Levi's theory, but the truth was, he didn't think his father was capable of loving anyone other than himself. Then again, maybe it had just been Lyndon and his mother his father had deemed unlovable. Try as he might, Lyndon couldn't believe the problem was him or his mother, not completely at least. His father had hated him on sight, without knowing him. How could it be something about Lyndon's personality, then, when his father hadn't a clue as to the kind of person Lyndon was?

"I just don't know, but I doubt it. I mean," Lyndon looked at Cheryl. "Could you imagine hating one of your kids enough to threaten to kill them if they didn't run far away? Would your territory mean so much you'd murder one of them?"

Cheryl was shaking her head before Lyndon finished. "No, never. In someone who'd do so, there would be more beast than man, don't you think? But you aren't like him, controlled by your cougar, otherwise you wouldn't be sitting here conversing with a bunch of other cats. And you said that guy, Grady, he took you in and helped you out. So I think it's clear there are cougar shifters who are just as capable as we are of letting the man control the beast. I don't think your father cared to do so."

# Chapter Seventeen

Levi couldn't imagine either of his parent's being anything other than the loving people they'd always been. For that matter, his entire family, cousins, aunts and uncles included, were very close and supportive. Being gay was a non-issue, he and Oscar, as well as their cousins and uncle who were gay, were all treated the same as everyone else. He did wonder if Lyndon's father hated him because of his sexuality, but he couldn't comprehend the man doing so.

"Does he know?" Levi asked.

Lyndon frowned and canted his head to the side. "Does he know what?"

"That you're gay?"

"I don't think so. I'd only just figured it out myself right before my mother passed away. I hadn't even done anything—never had a boyfriend or anyone to mess around with when my father showed up. I think he just hates me because I exist."

Oscar growled as he flopped back in his chair. "What an ass—"

"Oscar David Travis, watch your mouth!" Cheryl admonished, sending her son a scalding look.

Oscar cringed and slunk further down in his seat. "Yes ma'am. Sorry." Oscar glanced at his mom. "But you have to admit, calling the guy a jerk is just not accurate. He's way worse than a guy who says he'll call and doesn't, which is jerk-level as far as I'm concerned. Levi called him a jerk earlier but he's just nicer than I am."

Cheryl didn't let up on the glare she was sending his way. "Be that as it may, I won't have cursing at the table."

"So if I get up—"

Henry reached over and popped Oscar, eliciting a yelp from the younger man. "Stop smarting off before I take you outside and tan your hide. I don't care if you're eighteen, I'm still your dad and Cheryl is still your mom and you will respect our rules."

"Yes, sir." Oscar rubbed at his head.

Levi had to bite his cheek to keep from snickering, and Orion and Drake seemed to be doing the same thing. There was no way the remaining brothers wanted to be cuffed upside the head or scolded like a wayward child as Oscar had been. Levi peeked at Lyndon and saw his lover was managing to keep a straight face, but Levi could feel his amusement. Levi turned his attention back to his mom when she cleared her throat.

"Are you sure the cougar who's been following you isn't your father?" Cheryl asked Lyndon.

"Doesn't smell like him," Lyndon said, "and he didn't bother playing games with me before. He was very direct, punctuated his threat by beating the tar out of me. Used his claws, too," Lyndon added, touching the right side of his ribs.

Levi hadn't yet got to lick every inch of Lyndon's body, but he would, and if he found scars there where Lyndon was rubbing... Well, he'd just have to do everything he could to help eradicate the bad memories associated with that area.

His mom continued asking questions. "And you've no idea who else it could be?"

Lyndon stopped fidgeting and gripped the edge of the table instead. "No, ma'am, I really don't. Like I told y'all, the only other cougar I've ever met was Grady, and he died. My mother was human, but she did know what I was." Lyndon sucked in a breath then exhaled slowly. "Most of the time, at least. Sometimes when she wasn't stable, she'd forget, I think." Lyndon shook himself as if shaking off the memories from the past. "Anyway, I couldn't even tell you if I have brothers and sisters. It isn't like I could ask."

"The scent isn't familiar at all to you?"

Levi perked up at the question, because there was just a hint of something important in his mother's voice.

Lyndon mulled it over for a moment before answering. "I—it's hard to say. The scent is definitely familiar to me now, but I'd think that's because I've been smelling it for months."

"His senses aren't as acute as ours when he's not in his cougar form," Levi pointed out, then thought to add, "and he shifts a lot faster than we can. I don't know if that's due to his breed of cat or what."

Cheryl appeared thoughtful for a moment, her gaze distant as she tapped a rhythmic beat on the tabletop. "Hmm. I don't know either, but both things are interesting. I wish we had someone we could ask

## Levi

about such differences. Do you know if the cougars you've met shift as fast as you do?"

"Yeah." Lyndon offered. "My father and Grady were both at least as fast to shift as I am."

Levi thought now might be the best time for him to add a bit more about the differences between cougar and snow leopard shifters. "I think it might be breed specific." And now he had everyone's undivided attention. Lyndon's intense gaze was going to distract Levi if he wasn't careful, so Levi reluctantly looked away, staring at his mom instead. "I can sort of sense some of what Lyndon is feeling, but he can't do the same to me."

Lyndon smiled crookedly, making Levi's heart thud a rapid beat. "No, I can't, but I can read your expressions. You say a lot without even speaking."

"Levi's always been an open book," Henry chimed in, grinning at him. "Which might explain why we saw so little of him this past week." He narrowed his eyes and his grin vanished. "And we are going to have a talk about that, young man. I can't believe you didn't tell us about meeting Lyndon."

Levi was sure his entire face was neon pink. He couldn't imagine anyone wanting to tell their parents about a one-off with a stranger. He'd known his family would pick up on him being in a funk and hound the truth out of him, which was why he'd spent almost every waking hour working or in the woods—well, and because he was hoping to see Lyndon again.

Lyndon gave his hand a reassuring squeeze. "I imagine he didn't want to have to tell you about what we did. What happened between us was definitely personal, and to be truthful, I handled it badly."

Oscar snorted and Levi glared at his brother. "Don't start."

Cheryl turned to Oscar. "You knew about it and didn't say anything." It wasn't a question, and Levi couldn't help but think if Oscar slunk any further in his seat, he'd be under the table. "Don't think you aren't in trouble, too, son."

Levi shot Oscar a sympathetic look before turning his attention back to his mom. "It's my fault, Mom. He was just doing what I begged him to do."

"Right," Cheryl scoffed, but the way she smiled implied she wasn't truly angry. "Because we *all* know Oscar is such a malleable young man, never expressing an opinion of his own, unable to think for himself—" She broke off as she laughed, and Levi couldn't blame her.

The description of Oscar was so inaccurate it defied logic. And while Oscar tended to be quiet and avoid most people, he wasn't standoffish with his family—at least not his immediate family.

"No, I think he did what he wanted to do, Levi. You didn't twist his arm."

Oscar grumbled about being perfectly capable of making up his own mind and Levi let the subject drop. Coddling his brother wasn't something Levi did, not if he wanted to keep Oscar from feeling like Levi perceived him as being weak. As sensitive as Oscar was about his missing fingertips and his shorter stature, Levi was careful not to do anything that would further erode Oscar's confidence.

Lyndon squirmed beside him, placing their hands on Levi's thigh. Levi caressed the back of Lyndon's hand, hoping the small touch would offer some comfort. Lyndon was feeling guilty, blaming himself for Levi and Oscar's ass-chewing that was sure to come. Levi leaned closer and nuzzled Lyndon's cheek, not bothering to whisper when he spoke but still keeping his voice soft. "Oscar and I both made our own choices. No reason for you to feel bad about it."

"Exactly," his dad stated firmly. "Our boys know they are responsible for their actions and words. Now"—Henry looked at Lyndon sternly—"I don't particularly like how you ran off and left Levi, but considering your...meeting up...must have been intense and afterwards, frightening, I can understand it." Levi found himself the recipient of and even sterner look from his dad. "And it isn't like Levi bothered to go after you."

Which was only the truth, so there wasn't any point in arguing.

Henry sat back and considered them while Cheryl took over the conversation. "As for the bond you two have together, well, I haven't seen anything quite like it before. I wonder if it's because you are both shifters. None of the rest of the family is married to or dating other breeds of shifters. It would be weird if they were with shifters since the only ones we've known up 'til now was family."

"That kind of makes sense," Levi said, thinking it the most likely explanation. "Maybe like our instincts helped us find the one person we were meant to be with, instead of having to wait and see if we'd fit." Then he wanted to melt into the chair when it dawned on him what he'd just said. He'd pretty much proclaimed he and Lyndon were going to be a lifetime couple. Stupid, considering they didn't know each other and—

Lyndon's hand on the back of his neck caused Levi's panic to ramp up another notch. Levi wasn't aware of anything else just then besides Lyndon's touch, and he forced himself to look at the man, afraid he'd find anger or disbelief in his expression. But what he found rocked the edges of his soul and warmed him to the darkest pits of his being.

Lyndon's eyes glowed, a fondness in them that promised a future and life together. The brush of his lips over Levi's soothed his fears. He parted his lips and let Lyndon in, shivering when Lyndon's tongue speared into his mouth.

"Uh, guys?"

Oscar's smug voice penetrated the lusty fog swamping Levi's brain. Lyndon growled softly, an acknowledgement maybe, but he didn't end the kiss right away. Instead he sucked Levi's bottom lip and laved it thoroughly, turning Levi into a nearly boneless, horny heap of need.

Levi's cheeks were burning but not from embarrassment when the kiss ended. Desire was heating him from the inside out. He yearned to bend over the table and give himself to Lyndon—except not when his family was anywhere near.

"Reminds me of us," his mom murmured, and Levi risked a glance since she sounded happy rather than irritated at their display.

Levi had half expected to get lectured on proper table manners, and it had nothing to do with the fact that he was being kissed by a man. He'd have expected any of his siblings to be told to show some restraint no matter what sex their partner was. But his mother was smiling softly at his dad, who was nodding and looking back at Cheryl in a way that made Levi want to run his parents out of his home. The desire between the two of them had always been evident, as had their love, but still, there were just some things children never wanted to think about—such as their parents doing the deed.

Lyndon's quiet chuckle had Levi turning to him instead while Drake told his parents to get a room. "It's good knowing your parents love each other. Mine obviously didn't. I told you about our one and only meeting. He said some horrible things about my mom then, things that hurt worse than his claws or teeth, worse than his hatred of me. From what he said about my mother, I wonder why he ever deigned to speak to her in the first place."

"What do you mean?" Levi asked, although he thought he knew.

Lyndon's answer confirmed Levi's suspicions.

"He said she was a crazy bi—" Lyndon stopped short and cast an apologetic glance at Cheryl. "Er, he said she was crazy and should have killed herself before she ever had me. And if he'd known how unstable she was, he'd never have had sex with her. Then he told me I would end up just as crazy as she had been, but I'd do it out of his territory. There wasn't much else said then. He just shoved a cheque in my jeans pocket after he tore into me then he left."

"Jesus," Levi whispered, aching for Lyndon. "You told us about that last night, and it still shocks me hearing it again. You're lucky he didn't kill you."

Lyndon shrugged as he pushed back his chair. "Guess he figured he was right—but he wasn't, obviously. I don't have the same mental illness my mother had. Excuse me." He stood and started clearing off the dishes.

Levi and his brothers rose and began clearing the table as well.

# Chapter Eighteen

After cleaning the kitchen, Lyndon caught Levi's hand in his and followed Henry out back. The scent hit Lyndon first, which meant it was strong since he had such dulled senses as a man. Then he saw the tracks, paw prints and places where another cougar had scratched, leaving his mark. The foul odour of faeces and urine made Lyndon's eyes water and he could only begin to imagine how much worse it must be for Levi and his family with their more finely tuned senses.

"There's scratches on these trees, too." Orion pointed to several of the trees on the backside of the cabin's yard. "This really pisses me off. He comes in here, marking his territory! *His* territory! What does he think we are, a bunch of pussies?"

"Orion," Henry snapped, glaring at a particularly deep gouge on a tree. He ran his finger over it and appeared to grow angrier. "Yes, it's an insult to us all, and a direct challenge to Lyndon. While I'd love nothing more than to catch the fucker, we need to let Lyndon decide the next move—for now."

"Language, Dad," Drake said smartly, only to turn repentant when Henry whirled on him. "Sorry, sir. Mom's not here, though, so—"

"You're mom's hearing is sharp enough she probably heard us both and you know it! And I'm still your dad even if we aren't at the table," Henry pointed out, "You'd do well to keep your smart comments to yourself unless you want to be helping your mom do all the cooking for the next month. Besides which, Oscar was right. Jerk just doesn't cover it. Whoever this guy is, he's much worse than just a jerk."

Cheryl came back from where she'd been tracking the cougar. She gestured at Lyndon. "Anything familiar about this scent?"

Lyndon saw the expectation in the man's eyes. He took a deep breath, as did everyone else standing out back. The cougar's scent was the same as the one who'd been following him. *Was that what Cheryl meant?*

"It's the same shifter whose been hunting me," he offered, but Cheryl only arched a brow at him. "What? What am I missing?" He sniffed again, as did everyone but Cheryl. Then Levi stiffened beside him.

Lyndon glanced at him, hoping for a clue.

"Shift," Levi suggested.

"All right." Lyndon only hesitated a few seconds before stripping. Cheryl turned away and everyone else was male. No need to be embarrassed, he reasoned. No one objected, so Lyndon didn't have a problem with it, plus it might be good for them to see how quickly he shifted in comparison to them.

Lyndon dropped to his hands and knees, transforming almost instantly. He saw the stunned expressions on Oscar, Drake and Henry's faces, then

Cheryl's when she faced him. He wasn't certain he could smile in this form, but he was sure trying.

Then Cheryl walked over and touched his nose. Lyndon inhaled and the offensive scent of the other cougar made him want to kill the trespasser. He hissed and found the tracks left on the ground, covering each one up, clawing the earth to help cover the other's scent. The trees he marked, rising up on his haunches and finding his reach surpassed the trespasser's, which made him purr happily.

The urine scent he covered after an almost apologetic glance at the others, who merely urged him to get it done. But the scat? He wasn't going to leave his mess on top of that one. He glared at the offensive stuff and snarled.

"Drake's going to get a shovel," Levi said, and Lyndon felt a little less pissed, but not much. "Lyndon, pay close attention to the actual scent of the other cougar. Can't you smell—"

"Levi, let him have a minute to think about it."

Levi didn't look happy about it but he followed his mom's advice—or order. Lyndon suspected it wasn't really advice at all. Lyndon closed his eyes and drew the other's odour into his lungs, past his nasal tissues still burning from the foul aroma. The smell was familiar, he'd caught whiffs of it off and on for months, so what was it Henry and Levi expected him to figure out now? He smelt the cougar even though he'd marked over the other's offensive leavings. But there was something—Lyndon opened his eyes and shifted, freaked out by the recognition once it slammed into him.

The scent was familiar, yes, and he'd never paid close enough attention before. Always he'd thought he was picking up his own scent—and why wouldn't he?—along with his stalker's. And he was, to an extent, but the familiarity was not all just his own odour he was catching, but the link he'd so blindly ignored, and he wasn't sure it wasn't on purpose.

He turned to Levi and stumbled to his lover, shock coursing in his veins. "How could I not have known?"

Levi stroked his back, his sides, placing soft kisses on his temple and cheek. "Because he smells sort of like you. Maybe you didn't want to admit it, either. I don't think I'd be able to handle it, knowing one of my brother's was trying to hunt me down."

Just hearing it said made Lyndon ache all the way down to his feet. "I didn't even know I had a brother. I mean, I thought my father had probably knocked up other women, I knew there was a chance, of course. But I didn't *know*!"

The similarity in his scent and the other shifter's was definitely there, so why hadn't he noticed it before? Was it because the cougar shifter smelt enough like Lyndon's own scent, that he'd just assumed he was mixing their scents? He hadn't thought to concentrate on the odour, he hadn't thought—and now, the idea was right there in front of him. He had a sibling, at *least* one, and that his mystery brother was hunting him? It was like being ripped open all over again. It fucking hurt, and Lyndon didn't know how to deal with it.

"Let's go inside," Levi murmured, slipping an arm around Lyndon's waist.

Lyndon leaned heavily on him, his mind racing and his heart aching as he wondered why his family was so screwed up. His mother had been unstable more often than not, and his father had hated him. Now, apparently, he had a half-brother who hated him enough to stalk and terrorise him across the damn country.

Lyndon tried to pull away but Levi held on tight so he couldn't break the hold without possibly hurting one or both of them. "I need to see if he's still out here somewhere—"

Henry placed a hand on his back, startling Lyndon to silence. As Lyndon looked into Henry's eyes, eyes almost the same shade of pale green as Levi's, he saw so much affection and concern there it made his throat ache.

"No, you two go on inside and let Cheryl and my other boys handle it. The scent is hours old, and I doubt the jackass who did this is still around, but, you need to understand something." Henry smiled and gripped the back of Lyndon's neck firmly, in a way that brought comfort rather than panic. "You're family now, unless you were planning on leaving Levi?"

"No," Lyndon blurted out, almost shouting the word. "I won't, but—"

Henry held up his other hand. "Then no arguing. You let us help. Cheryl, Drake, Orion and Oscar can check out the woods behind here. I'll do what I can at home, which is probably going to be researching Cole Tavares online. We'll come back after we're done and tell you what we found, if we find anything. Then we're gonna sit down and figure out, together, what we need to do, okay?"

Lyndon didn't think he could get a word out around the lump in his throat, so he settled for a nod and blinked away the burning in his eyes. Henry let go of his neck and patted him on the back a few times.

"Let me just get out dishes and such out of the kitchen," Henry said as he strode past them, his other sons right behind him. Cheryl started to follow but paused at the door. She winked at Lyndon. "It'll be all right." She then kissed his cheek before going inside.

Lyndon didn't think anyone besides Grady had ever been so kind to him, and it touched him and thawed a small piece of his heart he'd thought had died long ago. The idea that he could truly have all of this, Levi and a family too, was almost unbelievable. But it was very real, and he vowed to himself no to do anything to fuck it up or let any of these incredible people get hurt.

After a minute or two of Levi murmuring soothing words in his ear, Lyndon and Levi made their way inside. Oscar hovered in the kitchen, his hands clamped together as he watched them. Lyndon found it hard to look at Levi's brother, even though he kind of liked the little blond. It might have been petty of him, but the bond between Levi and Oscar made Lyndon want to break down and cry for his own fucked-up family.

"Can I do anything to help?"

"I thought you were going out with Dad and the others."

"I am, I just wanted to make sure you know I'd help in any way I can. And I needed to stop by my place first. I have to feed my fish." Oscar appeared to be so earnest Lyndon didn't doubt the man at all.

Lyndon almost snickered at that, a leopard having fish, but he didn't quite have the energy to do so. He was tired, and there were so many conflicting emotions zipping through him. The way he felt about his genetic family — except his mother, he'd loved her even though she hadn't always been able to take care of him — and the way he felt for his possibly new family were overwhelming him at the moment.

Levi stopped by the table, bringing his other arm around Lyndon as he stepped in front of him. "We're good, Oscar. Just be careful when you go back to your cabin. We don't know where the other cougar is."

"Okay, but you'll call me if you need anything, right?"

Lyndon could feel Oscar's gaze on him, and he wanted to squirm. He wasn't used to so many people giving a shit about him. He wished he could say something let Oscar know he'd be okay, but Lyndon ached inside, like he was raw and bleeding in a way he hadn't experienced since his mother's death and his father's attack.

"Of course we will," Levi told his brother. "We're just going to lie down for a while." He hesitated a second before adding, "Maybe you should stay here, watch TV in the living room or something."

Even as wrecked as Lyndon was, he knew Oscar wasn't going to handle the suggestion well. Oscar proved him right when the younger man stomped—Lyndon couldn't see him since Oscar was behind him, but each of Oscar's footsteps made the wood floors vibrate—over to their sides.

"I am *not* a helpless little twink," Oscar snapped.

Lyndon turned his head and was impressed by the furious expression twisting Oscar's cute features.

Then Oscar raised his hand and wiggled his damaged fingers at Levi. "And *this* doesn't make me helpless! It just makes me freaking gross! But that doesn't mean I can't walk a whole two hundred yards to my cabin, and it sure as hell doesn't mean I can't go out with my father and brothers to see if we can find the asshole who stank up your back yard!"

## Levi

Levi had gone taut against Lyndon, and now he was wound so tight Lyndon half expected him to snap in two.

"I never said you were helpless or any of the other crap you're going on about," Levi gritted out. "I just want you to be careful! In the wild, cougars are very aggressive and territorial—"

"I know what they're like! I researched them right after you told me about Lyndon! But we aren't in the wild, and we aren't wild cats! And besides," Oscar turned his fierce gaze on Lyndon before going on, "has this dude hurt anyone? Or is he just chasing you? Maybe he only wanted your attention."

"He got it, and no, he hasn't hurt anyone, as far as I know. But that doesn't mean anything. There was never anyone I cared about before, once my mom and Grady died." Lyndon wasn't going to explain the threat he felt. Oscar was a smart guy, he had to know all the shit out back hadn't been a cry for attention. It'd been a threat, a promise. "He's telling me he's tired of playing. I don't think he's intending to come say hello to his long-lost brother. He could have done so any time over the past months. You *know* that, Oscar, so give Levi a break. He's right to be concerned about *all* of us."

"But—" Oscar began.

Lyndon straightened his spine and stepped away from Levi. "But nothing! If this cougar," he couldn't quite bring himself to call the man his brother, half-brother, *whatever*, "if he decides to attack, it won't be like anything you've ever known. It won't be a playful tussle or a bit of roughhousing where he stops when you cry uncle." Lyndon took another step closer to Oscar, willing the younger man to understand and believe him.

"He won't take it easier on you because you're smaller, or because of this—" Lyndon touched Oscar's damaged hand. "He will use everything he has to take you down, and I don't know—I'm afraid nothing will stop him until you've bled out or he's snapped your neck from behind like cougars are apt to do. So don't...don't blow off Levi's concern. Don't get all pissed because he loves you. Be fucking glad he *does*, because I can tell you, it sucks beyond all words and hurts like you wouldn't believe to be the recipient of the exact opposite of a brother's love. Because that out there? That was hate, pure and simple."

Oscar's expression had changed from angry to remorseful during Lyndon's rant, and now he closed the distance between them and hugged Lyndon, his embrace surprisingly strong. "You can be my brother. I won't ever treat you like I hate you."

Lyndon smiled for the first time since he'd stepped outside. "Guess I don't have to worry about the taxidermist, then."

# Chapter Nineteen

Oscar left and Levi watched, Lyndon at his side as they stood on the front porch. It was a straight shot from Levi's to Oscar's, and once his brother made it safely inside his house, and texted Levi letting him know all was well there, Levi relaxed. He also saw three snow leopards coming from the woods in front of Oscar's, which reassured him even more.

Assured Oscar was safe, Levi led Lyndon into the bedroom. He'd wanted to comfort Lyndon, wanted to love away all the pain he could feel rolling off him. Levi walked to the bathroom, his hand in Lyndon's. Once he got the shower started, he stripped then undressed Lyndon as well. He framed Lyndon's face with his hands and kissed him, a tender melding of lips and tongues, and it set Levi's heart to soaring with a soft, comforting joy.

"It will be okay," he promised, believing it in every bit of his being. "We will be okay, we'll be fine."

Before Lyndon could answer, Levi kissed him again. He ran his hands down the broad planes of Lyndon's chest then kissed a trail to his neck. Levi lapped at the thin skin covering Lyndon's pulse, then nibbled it just to make Lyndon shiver. Although, he did enjoy it too.

Lyndon palmed Levi's ass, kneading his cheeks as Levi scraped his teeth down to Lyndon's shoulder.

"Levi."

Lyndon hissed when Levi slowly lowered himself to his knees, kissing and nipping Lyndon's chest and stomach. Using his hands, he traced Lyndon's side, stopping when he felt a softer patch of skin between Lyndon's ribs on his right side.

Levi scooted over until he could see what he was feeling. Between Lyndon's last four ribs were thick silver scars where claws had torn flesh. Levi sucked in a breath at the sight.

"It wasn't so bad," Lyndon murmured, but his rough voice and the way his skin twitched under Levi's touch told a different story, as did the emotions Lyndon was battling back. "He could have killed me."

"He should have loved you." Levi pressed his cheek against the scars and wished he could absorb Lyndon's pain, erase the bad memories and years of hurt. "He never deserved to have you as a son. He's not good enough to be your dad."

Lyndon settled one hand on Levi's head, threading his fingers through his hair. "Levi, we need to—I need to figure out what to do about...about..."

"You had it right the first time." Levi tipped his head up, looking into Lyndon's gold eyes. "*We* need to figure out what to do, soon. But for now, I want to take care of you. Trust my family to watch out for us, and trust me—just trust me." Levi wanted that, wanted Lyndon to know he could always count on him.

Lyndon's breath was raspy when he cupped Levi's chin. The gold in his eyes seemed to warm and lighten, turning almost yellow as he stared down at Levi. "I do trust you, and your family."

Levi smiled so big it made his cheeks hurt. "Your family now. You're stuck with all of us."

Lyndon's smile in return was beaming. "They're the best gift I could ever have."

"You might not think so in a little less than a year." Levi snorted then nibbled on the tip of one of Lyndon's fingers when he rubbed at Levi's lip.

"What's going to happen in a little less than a year?"

Levi mock-shuddered and tried to make his eyes as big as he could. "The annual family reunion. It's held here every summer, a week of extended family visits. You're lucky since it just concluded the day we first met."

"Maybe we could take a vacation that week," Lyndon suggested, although he looked rather anticipatory.

"Grandma would skin us both."

There were some things you just weren't allowed to do, and skipping out on the family reunion was one of them. The other was exposing what they were to outsiders. The only time that was acceptable was if they knew whoever was being told loved them enough to keep their secret. Divorces didn't happen in the family, probably because every one of the shifters was very careful about choosing their partner. Or maybe there was more to it, like the shifters who had a serious and committed relationship with a human felt the exact same intrinsic sense of rightness as he felt for Lyndon. He'd have to ponder the issue another time.

"Speaking of skin..." Levi traced over the silvery scars on Lyndon's side then nipped him. "You taste so good."

The scent of Lyndon's arousal grew stronger and Levi used his other hand to fist Lyndon's cock. A couple of slow strokes and Lyndon's breaths became shaky pants.

"Jesus, I'm not going to last."

"Don't want you to," Levi muttered. He smoothed his other hand over the firm swell of Lyndon's ass. He traced the fuzzy trail in Lyndon's crease, his fingers brushing over Lyndon's hole. "Do you ever?"

Levi looked up when Lyndon didn't answer immediately. Golden eyes gleamed, warming him from the groin outward.

"I haven't." Lyndon buried his hands in Levi's hair. "I don't know if I can, or if I'd like it. But, I think maybe, if I cared about the person doing it and trusted them…"

Taking it for the suggestion it was, Levi pulled his hand away from Lyndon's butt. He brought his fingers to his mouth and sucked them, coating them well then, gaze locked on Lyndon's, Levi sought out his lover's tight little ring, pushing his fingertips against it.

Lyndon moaned and closed his eyes when Levi applied pressure to his opening, using just one digit. The tip slipped into Lyndon's silky warm hole and Levi had to use every bit of his self-control to keep from coming. He took his other hand and levelled Lyndon's cock to his mouth and sucked the wet tip in. Lyndon's salty taste flooded his senses, and Levi could no more stop the moan that tore up from his chest than he could have stopped the Titanic from sinking with an oar.

"Yes, damn it, Levi." Lyndon's grip tightened in his hair, holding Levi in place and thrusting his hips.

Levi whimpered needily, sucking hard and taking Lyndon's length into his mouth. The crown of Lyndon's cock pushed into his throat and Levi moved both of his hands, pumping his finger in and out of Lyndon's ass and grabbing onto Lyndon's hip bruisingly hard with the other.

Lyndon grunted and he buried his cock deeper. Levi swallowed rapidly, hoping the pulsing sensation of his throat muscles would drive Lyndon's control into the ground. He wanted Lyndon to pound into him, to leave him aching, feeling the remnants of the way he'd pleased Lyndon for hours afterwards.

*Do it do it do it!* Levi was screaming it in his mind. He pressed another finger into Lyndon's ass. Hot and oh so tight, Lyndon's channel gripped him fiercely. Levi couldn't imagine how good it'd feel to fuck Lyndon, but he sure wanted the chance to find out if the reality was as good — or better — than he expected.

Lyndon tugged and Levi sucked back up Lyndon's thick cock, grazing his teeth here and there. He twisted his wrist, searching for that spot nestled inside Levi's ass. This wasn't the best angle to reach it, but he thought —

"Fuck!" Lyndon roared, slamming his hips forward then jerking back, pushing his ass towards Levi's hand. "More!"

Levi couldn't even grin around the fat cock in his mouth, but he could give Lyndon what he was demanding. Levi rubbed over the little nub again and Lyndon's thighs quivered, his belly rippled. Lyndon's grip grew tighter and he shouted again, his control snapping. Levi moaned, his cock hard and dripping, his balls drawing up as Lyndon pumped into his mouth, his throat. Levi speared a third finger into Lyndon's pucker, hoping it wasn't too much. Judging by the sounds Lyndon made and the way he rocked back and forth between Levi's finger and mouth, he didn't think it was.

Curses and praises rolled off Lyndon's tongue almost at the same speed pre-cum leaked from his dick. Levi, aching and on edge, reached down and fisted his shaft. Pleasure shot through him at the touch. Lyndon tightened his hold and slid his cock into Levi's mouth, swiveling his hips once he was buried to the root. Levi pushed his fingers in deep, as far as he could reach and felt Lyndon's dick swell. He pumped his own length using rapid, harsh strokes. Lyndon's inner muscles clenched, his ring squeezing around Levi's fingers. Lyndon mewled and jerkilywithdrew just enough to spill his cum on Levi's tongue.

The taste of his lover would have been enough to set Levi off, but listening to the sounds he made, feeling the snug grip on his fingers, the way Lyndon's body shook and the scent of his skin, his cum — all of it combined to send Levi's climax spiralling out. Spunk shot from his cock. Pleasure blinded him with a brilliant white display behind his closed lids.

Levi felt so loose he wouldn't have been surprised to find out his bones had melted. He managed to ease his fingers out while he lapped at Lyndon's dick. Lyndon whimpered and pulled back, either his cock too sensitive for any touch or else seeking the fingers that had filled him. Maybe both, but Levi couldn't concentrate to figure it out.

He rapped his knuckles on the floor when he lowered his arm. The small bite of pain didn't register much. Levi let go of his softening dick and remained kneeling since his head was kind of swimming .

"Fuck," Lyndon muttered, joining Levi on the floor. He brought Levi to him with one arm around his shoulders.

Levi tipped his chin up and puckered his lips, then opened them for the kiss Lyndon bestowed upon him. Lyndon seemed determined to lick every bit of his cum from Levi's mouth. Levi pressed closer until he could feel Lyndon's heart beating, pounding, and he canted his head to the side to give them a better angle for the kiss.

Once Lyndon seemed satisfied he'd cleaned all of his flavour from Levi's mouth, he sighed against Levi's lips. The slight gust of air almost tickled Levi's overly sensitised lips. He opened his eyes and found himself the recipient of Lyndon's golden stare once again.

"What?" It was about the best he could manage considering he'd just come so hard he felt like he'd been turned inside out.

Lyndon smiled crookedly at him then peppered Levi's face with noisy, wet kisses. He stopped when he reached Levi's ear, where he nibbled on the lobe. Levi's cock slowly began to fill again then the blood rushed south at a dizzying speed. Lyndon murmured, "You know, I think I *can*—and I think I'll like it." He was even eager to feel Levi fucking him…but a little scared, too.

Levi's expression softened and he cupped Lyndon's cheek. He thumbed Lyndon's bottom lip, setting off little sparks of arousal in his gut.

"It's okay, we have time. We don't have to rush."

Lyndon could only hope Levi was right.

# Chapter Twenty

By the time his dad and brothers returned, Levi was as tense as Lyndon. The worry Lyndon felt was being absorbed by Levi and the two of them had paced the front porch for the last half hour. When Cheryl darted out of the treeline still in snow leopard form, Levi rushed to the front door and held it open. His mom, followed by Drake, Orion and Oscar padded in and headed straight for Levi's bedroom.

"Get whatever clothes you need from the dresser," Levi told them then took Lyndon's hand and guided them to the living room.

The creak of the leather cushions seemed freakishly loud when they sat on the couch. Levi rested his head against Lyndon's shoulder and stroked his thumb over Lyndon's knuckles.

"It'll be fine. I don't think they found the other cougar, considering no one was hurt."

The four leopards had not moved like they were injured, and their coats were clean except for a leaf here and there.

"I didn't smell anything, either, other than their usual scents."

Lyndon grunted and fidgeted, tapping a finger on his knee. Mewls that turned to groans coming from the bedroom told Levi his mom and brothers had shifted.

"They'll be out in a minute." Levi heard his dresser drawers being slammed shut and he hoped to hell there was nothing embarrassing in them. Had he left any of his sex toys in his dresser? He thought they were in the box in the closet, but sometimes he got lazy.

His mom came out first wearing a pair of Levi's sweats—way too long—and his T-shirt—also huge on her. Oscar was right behind him, almost as lost in Levi's clothes as Cheryl was.

"Drake and Orion will be going up to our house for supper."

Levi nodded at his mom, watching her closely while she sat in the recliner. Oscar perched on the arm of the couch. His bottom lip protruded slightly, a sure sign Levi's little brother wasn't happy.

Cheryl leant forward and braced her forearms on her thighs. "So, Lyndon, we did find a few mangled rabbits, but the shifter wasn't anywhere to be found."

"The fucker used something obnoxious smelling to cover up his scent," Oscar groused, crossing his arms over his chest. "We couldn't even find where he came onto our property."

"Oscar," Cheryl warned, shooting her youngest son a glare. "I was getting to that point." She turned back to them. "The cougar didn't just cover his trail, he sprayed some noxious scent everywhere. It masked his odour well and did a number on our noses. We couldn't even figure out where he crossed onto our property."

Oscar shifted on the arm of the couch. He rubbed his nose and gave Cheryl a pleading look.

Cheryl sighed and sat back. "Go ahead, otherwise you're going to keep looking at me like you are and I'll either cave or get mad at being manipulated."

"It's just because my nose still burns. I hope there won't be any permanent damage to our olfactory senses."

Levi sat up at that, the top of his head grazing Lyndon's chin. "Sorry," he muttered. "It won't, right? Do you know what he used?"

"No," Cheryl admitted. "It was a mix of things, chemicals. It reeked, but I don't think the damage is permanent. I'm going to have your dad do some looking online, see if he can figure it out. I should have told him we were back already, but we'll be going home in just a few minutes. I'm afraid he'll head out on his own over here if he knows we're back."

"I'm sorry," Lyndon said as he grew rigid beside Levi. "Maybe I should—"

"No! You should *not* leave!" Levi wasn't even going to let the man finish the sentence!

"Your family is in danger, Levi. Already their ability to scent has been fucked up. How can you think me being here is a good thing?" Lyndon scowled and Levi could feel Lyndon's desire to stay as well as his fear. "If I leave now, maybe the other cougar will also leave. Or I can go out, alone, and wait for him. Put an end to this once and for all."

Levi's heart did its best to thump right out of his chest and he shook his head. Cheryl stood and walked over to stand in front of them.

She placed a hand on her hip and narrowed her eyes at Lyndon. "And what makes you think I would sit back and be okay with that? This isn't just about you, it's about my sons, too. Levi, of course, but Oscar, Drake and Orion were out there too and don't think for one second they aren't pissed enough to skin that cat alive."

"It's still my problem," Lyndon growled. He stood up and waved towards the door. "I brought this trouble here and I'll—oomph!" Cheryl slammed a hand against Lyndon's chest, sending him sprawling back onto the couch. Then she pointed at Lyndon and wore such a fierce expression Levi wanted to promise to never piss his mom off again.

"You listen to me, Lyndon. As far as I'm concerned, you're family now, and you can't tell me you don't want that. I can see it in your eyes, the longing there every time you look at us!" Lyndon opened his mouth but Cheryl bent closer and thumped him on the chest. "Don't even start with me. You may think you're some big bad cougar, but I've got a good thirty years on you *and* I raised these boys. I've learned tricks for handling stubborn men, don't think I haven't!"

Lyndon's eyes had grown bigger as Cheryl ranted. Levi wondered how Lyndon's eye sockets held his eyeballs in place.

"But—but I'm not a kid! You can't tell me—" Lyndon shut his mouth, most likely realising as Levi did, Lyndon sounded like a belligerent son. "I mean, Cheryl, come on! Your family has already been hurt—"

"Please," Oscar scoffed, glaring at Lyndon. "It just burns, like when I need to sneeze, only a little stronger. Don't make us out to be a bunch of wusses."

Lyndon's cheeks darkened and he rubbed at his temple. Cheryl placed a hand on his shoulder and Levi felt Lyndon shiver, felt the hungry need for approval as it rose in Lyndon.

"I told you, you are family now," Cheryl re-emphasised. She touched Lyndon's cheek. "Family sticks together. Now, this cougar has really ticked me off, and I want to find him and make sure he doesn't hurt *any* of my boys again. Do you understand?"

Lyndon's resistance snapped, Levi felt it like a rubber band stretched too far.

"Yes ma'am, and…and thank you."

Cheryl nodded and patted Lyndon's cheek before looking at Levi. "He's a good one, son. Got all those protective instincts and trying to make sure no one else gets hurt. You two will take good care of each other."

Levi was about glowing from his mom's approval. Oh, he'd known they liked Lyndon, but still, hearing it said just rocked Levi's world. "Love you, Mom."

Cheryl smiled and the last lingering bit of anger vanished from her expression. "Love you too. Probably even end up loving Lyndon once he gets it through his head we want him here, no matter what." Lyndon sucked in a sharp breath as Cheryl continued. "Now, here's what we're going to do. We'll bring everyone back to our house and set up patrols around the place. Levi, you and Lyndon can have the basement room."

"Thank God," Oscar chirped, waggling his eyebrows. "Otherwise none of the rest of us would get any sleep!"

"Oscar!" Levi thundered right along with his mom.

Lyndon laughed. Levi looked at him questioningly.

"What? He's right. I don't even know how we're going to keep quiet enough if we're in the basement, what with y'all's heightened hearing and all."

Cheryl blanched and Oscar chortled while Levi tried to melt into the couch cushions. "Maybe we should just stay here." He had to admit Lyndon had a point, even if it was embarrassing.

"Maybe you two should just count on exercising some restraint," Cheryl said.

"I vote for gags. They're a type of restraint."

Levi, Lyndon and Henry looked at Oscar.

"What?" Oscar asked. "It was just a suggestion. It's not like I said they should use ball-gags. A simple bandana would do."

"Jesus," Levi muttered.

Cheryl pointed towards the bedroom. "Oscar, go see why your other brothers aren't out here yet!" She snapped the order out in a voice that brooked no argument.

Oscar practically leapt off the arm of the couch. "Yes, ma'am," he called out, hustling away.

Cheryl harrumphed and crossed her arms over her chest. "That boy, God. I don't know what we're going to do with him. He's got a smart mouth."

"I vote you send him off to a private school overseas," Levi suggested jokingly. He'd never be able to stop worrying if Oscar were to be sent away.

"You'd have Oscar withdrawals," Lyndon informed him. "And I like the guy. The whole gag idea—"

"Guh!" Levi slapped a hand to his forehead and closed his eyes. "Not when my mom is standing there!"

"Yes, please, spare me."

Levi peeked at his mom, expecting to see her looking uncomfortable, but Cheryl was grinning like a damned loon. Drake and Orion walked into the living room then, and Oscar was right behind them, grumbling to himself. Drake rubbed at his eyes and Orion yawned.

"Sorry, Mom, we fell asleep," Drake muttered, his voice sleep-raspy.

"They were curled up on Levi's—and I guess Lyndon's—bed." Oscar wrinkled his nose. "Good thing our sense of smell is screwed up, otherwise they would have probably noticed—"

"Go home," Cheryl ordered, cutting Oscar off. "You three boys stay together and text Levi as soon as you reach the house. I'll stay here while Levi and Lyndon gather a few things."

Levi stood up as his brothers left. He tugged on Lyndon's hand and stepped aside to give Lyndon room to stand.

"We'll make it quick, Mom."

At Cheryl's nod, Levi and Lyndon hurried to the bedroom. Levi wondered if they shouldn't take a few bandanas with them.

# Chapter Twenty-One

It didn't take long for Lyndon to pack—it wasn't like he had much, so he helped Levi, stuffing sweats and jeans and whatever else Levi handed him into a large duffel bag.

"Can't forget these."

Lyndon turned and just managed to catch the lube and the box of condoms. "You're lucky I'm quick with both hands."

"Not too quick," Levi said, leering at Lyndon. "I happen to think your hands work at the perfect speed for me."

Lyndon's cock began to harden but he was not going to give in to his hormones! "No teasing me, Levi. Your mom is in the living room. Talk about a major cock block."

"No kidding." Levi tossed a pair of balled-up socks to Lyndon once he'd tucked away the other supplies.

Lyndon bit his lip then glanced at Levi. Now was one of the times he wished he could pick up on what his lover was feeling because he couldn't see past Levi's scowl to the cause of it beneath. Exhaling, he tried to word the questions in his head first then he decided to just ask. "Are you mad about us having to go stay at your folks' place? Do you wish we hadn't—"

That was as far as he got. Levi grabbed his shoulder and spun him around. Before Lyndon could do more than start to snarl, Levi kissed him eagerly, so eagerly in fact, their teeth clacked together. The coppery tang of blood reached Lyndon's tongue, the taste familiar— Levi's. Lyndon pulled back and lapped at Levi's lip. When he sucked on the split flesh, Levi moaned. Cheryl's shout for them to hurry up and quit messing around had Lyndon and Levi springing apart from one another.

"Packing," Lyndon rasped. "Right."

They finished up quickly then went into the living room where Cheryl was waiting, tapping one foot in a rapid *tat tat tat*. "I thought I might have to come get you two." She shuddered and gestured to the door. "Let's go."

Levi locked up the house once they were outside on the porch.

Cheryl looked off towards her house then back at Levi. "Did Oscar text you yet?"

"Um." Levi handed Lyndon the duffle then dug his cell phone out of his back pocket.

Cheryl took the phone and pressed a button, the bright light from the screen illuminating her features as she scowled at it.

Lyndon heard it a second after Levi did. There was a faint whistling then Cheryl grunted and dropped the phone.

"Shit! Get down!" Lyndon leapt, arms wide to encircle Levi and Cheryl both.

## Levi

He took them down, Henry not making a sound as they hit the wooden porch floor. Levi cursed then grunted as the breath whooshed from his lungs. His cell phone lay several feet away on the ground beyond the front porch steps.

"What happened?" Levi whispered, the words barely audible. "Mom? Mom!"

"Quiet." Lyndon could feel Cheryl's heart beating, felt her breath against his cheek. "She's alive. Stay down for now but get her and yourself inside as soon as I distract this fucker."

"Come out and play, Lyndon. I've grown tired of chasing you around the country." The challenge in the deep, mocking voice was unmistakable.

It sent chills over Lyndon's skin as anger churned in his gut.

Lyndon kept quiet and hoped to whatever gods existed Levi would do the same. He held a hand up in the direction where Levi and Cheryl lay, trying to convey his wish for them to remain silent. When a few seconds had passed with no one making a sound, Lyndon took a step back then began moving along the front of the house. He had to duck before reaching the window, not wanting the light from inside to give away his movements. The other cougar shifter's next words caused Lyndon to stumble as fear iced his veins.

"Do you want to know what I did to those other three pussies?"

Levi's muffled sob broke Lyndon's heart. He turned his head and just made out the dark shape of his lover. Knowing Levi could pick up on his emotions, Lyndon tried to send waves of comfort and reassurance to Levi. He needed Levi to stay here, to be safe.

"They aren't dead yet, but if you don't get out here, they will be. A bullet to the brain will kill a shifter just as it would a human."

Lyndon stopped worrying about trying to move unnoticed as another of those heart-rending sounds came from Levi. Lyndon ran, slapping a hand down on the railing and leaping over it to land beside the porch. He headed in the direction of the voice had come from. The asshole was downwind of them, which was why they hadn't scented him.

Pulling off his clothes was difficult since he didn't want to stop moving, and Lyndon finally thought, *fuck it,* and shifted in mid-stride. He landed hard; his back legs tangled in his pants but Lyndon quickly freed himself. His senses sharpened and he saw the person who'd been stalking him—and gasped in surprise.

*Could have been my twin.* The sick grin on the man's face stretched wider. He laid down what Lyndon thought was some sort of tranquilizer gun, maybe. Then he shifted, too and yowled a challenge. Lyndon dug in his back claws and threw himself forward to meet it.

The scent of blood, more than one person's, fuelled Lyndon's fury even. He didn't want to have to kill his own kin, but the human and cat both knew he'd probably have no other choice. Lyndon locked down his emotions before he let them get in the way of what had to be done. The cat surged towards him, snarling, teeth bared and eyes flashing. Lyndon called on his cougar instincts, letting them override his human ones. There was no way he could bring this to an end without more violence, he needed to remember that. Talking wouldn't work against a man who was more beast than human. There was nothing in his attacker's eyes signifying an intelligence other than the cat's.

The shrill scream he let out when he leapt was matched by his foe's. They slammed into one another, claws and teeth tearing at whatever part of each other they could reach. Neither had their legs fully under them when they hit the ground. Instead they rolled and fought for position. Lyndon felt a searing pain in his shoulder when he twisted his neck, trying to sink his teeth into the cougar. He curled his paw and tore into the flesh of his haunches.

His opponent snarled and swatted at him, catching the tender tip of his nose. Lyndon yelped, unable to keep the sound in. The twinge of pain and embarrassment powered him forward when the cougar retreated. Lyndon dug in his back claws and pushed off. He tackled the shifter, knocking him on his back. His side was raked with sharp claws and spots danced before his eyes. Lyndon did his best to ignore it, shoving his head down, finding the vulnerable arch of his foe's neck—only to have him shift into human form.

"Please," the man rasped, his hands shaking against Lyndon's sides. "I only came after you because our father made me."

He should have suspected, Lyndon thought, but no, he'd left like his father had told him to and assumed as long as he stayed out of south Texas...

"It's in his will, when he dies only the surviving heir gets everything."

Lyndon stumbled off the man, stunned by his father's depravity—and his half-brother's. The man didn't have to go along with this sick shit. Lyndon watched his...brother...pant, saw his chest heaving. Blood streamed from a dozen wounds, and Lyndon knew he wasn't in much better shape. What sympathy he felt was squashed by the memory of his brother's gloating threat to kill Oscar, Drake and Orion. Lyndon remembered the scent of blood—not his, not this man who shared his blood but wasn't family, could never be when he'd so willingly and gleefully hunted Lyndon.

He didn't make a sound when he straddled the gasping form on the ground. Lyndon locked his gaze to the man's then bared his teeth in a silent growl. Then he tipped his head and, sore nose or not, used it to smack the underside of his would-be killer's chin. The man arched his neck and grabbed at him, but Lyndon ignored him and opened his mouth. He didn't bite too deeply, his teeth barely digging into the skin. Lyndon growled, letting his anger and pain flow into the sound. His threat was clear, real—he'd rip the man's throat out without hesitation. And later, he'd mourn and live with the regret, but no one other than him needed to know about it. *But Levi would know.*

Lyndon didn't want to expose his lover to that kind of pain, even if it was secondary, coming from Lyndon. He couldn't let this man beneath him know it, not if he wanted this to end without death. He needed to think Lyndon would kill him without regret if Lyndon had any hope at all of making him back down and submit. Lyndon clenched his jaw enough to sink the tips of his teeth in a little more. The taste of his own sibling's blood sickened him, and he had to lock his muscles in place to keep from heaving.

Beneath him, his brother was utterly still, barely daring to breathe. His fear singed Lyndon's sinuses and didn't bring him the slightest pleasure. When his prey had been still for a full minute, showing his submission, Lyndon released him and backed away slowly, not wanting to appear weak or eager to get away from what he'd just done.

He wanted to look for Oscar and the other two brothers, wanted to make sure Levi and Cheryl were okay, but he didn't dare take his eyes off the downed man. Lyndon growled a soft warning when his half-brother pushed himself up to a sitting position.

"My name is Albert," he said as he tried to get his legs underneath him. Since there was a wound running down from his buttocks to his thigh on the right side, Lyndon doubted Albert could stand. "It's supposed to make it harder to kill someone, isn't it? Knowing their name?"

Lyndon didn't think it could get any harder than it already was. The very idea of having to kill anyone was repulsive, but killing a brother he might have — had their father not been such a cruel bastard — been close to, like Levi and his brothers were? It hurt, a physical pain that he felt in his bones.

Albert gave up on standing and began scooting backwards. Lyndon hoped he was just trying to put a little more space between them.

"You know, there are more than just me. I'm not the only cub our father actually raised."

Albert's words were like metal spikes piercing Lyndon to his soul. Would he have to fight more siblings, maybe even kill them? All for a fucking empire founded on oil and hatred? His father wasn't the biggest name in the oil industry in south Texas, but he damned sure was wealthy and renowned.

"There's probably a few more bastards, like you," Albert continued, still moving away. "Father wasn't particularly faithful. Guess he wanted to spread his seed and make sure he had one suitable successor. If there are, I'll have to kill them first, of course."

The words shattered in Lyndon's mind because they were so incomprehensible. The realisation sunk in then; Albert wouldn't stop. He didn't even sound the least bit remorseful. Lyndon couldn't just let him go, knowing he might have siblings out there with targets on the backs of their necks. Yet he couldn't quite bring himself to leap, to tear into Albert's neck and put an end to this nightmare.

"You don't like that, do you? But it's the way it is. Just be glad you weren't raised by our father." Albert's bitter laugh carried so much pain Lyndon started trying to think of alternatives to killing him.

Then Albert grinned and he pulled something from behind his back. The moonlight glinted off metal. Albert aimed the gun at him, and Lyndon was afraid he'd made a fatal mistake.

# Chapter Twenty-Two

He couldn't stand it anymore. Yes, Lyndon had pretty much told Levi to stay and wait like a good little wife... Well, he wasn't doing that. Once he'd pulled the freaking dart thingie from his mom's shoulder and seen she would be okay, the need to get to Lyndon was all but irresistible.

At least, he hoped his mom would be okay. After about five minutes, Cheryl had groaned and her eyelids had fluttered open before dropping closed again. But her breathing was steady, deep, her heartbeat strong. Levi really thought his mom would be fine.

Lyndon, however... Levi could hear the snarling, the yowls of pain, some Lyndon's, some not. He absolutely couldn't stay here, but if he left and something happened to his dad, Levi didn't think he could live with himself.

"Go. Go on."

Levi startled at hearing his mom's voice. He'd been looking at the front door, thinking about what he should do. He'd got his mom inside, and Lyndon was out there. Oscar... Oscar, Orion and Drake might be hurt, lying bloody and in pain somewhere. Or worse, they might be dead.

He turned to Chery; and touched her slightly lined face. Then he pressed a hand over her heart. "Are you sure, Mom? I don't know if leaving you—"

"I'm fine," his mom grumbled, shoving herself up on her elbows. She seemed steady although beads of sweat sprouted on her forehead. "Nothing is hurting inside, or numb, like I was poisoned. Just felt a sting then not much else. Like I passed out. Go on and find your brothers, and make sure Lyndon isn't hurt. I'll be along as soon as I can."

Levi started to leave then a thought chilled him to the core. "Mom, what about Dad?"

He hadn't ever seen his mom move so fast. Levi turned away quickly as Cheryl started pulling off her clothes. He barely made it to the front door in time to open it. He'd been afraid his mom was going to try to go through the damn thing instead. Levi did hesitate on the porch, torn between concern for his parents and for his brothers and Lyndon.

Then he felt it, Lyndon's fear, his sorrow, his certainty that he had failed. And Levi ran, not bothering to shift. He didn't have the time to spare. Stones and sticks bruised and gouged his feet but the pain was negligible in comparison to his fear for Lyndon Lyndon had headed downwind, so Levi couldn't scent as much as he'd have been able to otherwise, but he did smell blood the closer he got to where Lyndon was. When he realised some of it was his brothers' blood, Levi bit his tongue to hold back the anguished roar building inside him.

And when he came close enough to see the fucker pointing a gun at Lyndon, heard the hammer being

## Levi

pulled back, he had never felt so useless. His shout died on his tongue as he realised he might startle the man into firing the gun. Levi wondered why they hadn't heard him coming, but the two seemed so locked into whatever was happening between them, which might have been his answer. He crept forward quietly, listening intently as the armed man spoke.

"Now, obviously you aren't the superior son. You're weak, unable to do what needs to be done. I thought I might be too, at first, but the thrill of playing around, of tormenting you—don't all cats like to toy with their prey? It was addictive. If you hadn't decided to stay here and ruin my fun, I might have let you live a little longer."

The man tapped his chin while he hummed. "Now, do I want to kill the man, or the cougar? Why don't you shift back and forth and I'll just shoot whenever I get the urge? We'll see which one I get—although, I am killing both, but still." He laughed while never taking his attention off Lyndon. "Better get started or else I'll go back and put a bullet in every one of those idiots' heads. Then I'll kill the guy you've been fucking, after I fuck him, of course. Think he'll scream for me like he did for you? I heard it all the way out in the woods."

Lyndon shifted then, from cougar to man. "Albert, please—"

*Don't beg, don't fucking beg for anything from that bastard!* Levi willed Lyndon to hear him, but Lyndon stopped anyway when Albert raised the gun slightly and pulled the trigger. The bullet sent bark flying out, bits of wooden shrapnel pelting Lyndon and tearing at his skin.

"Shut the fuck up, bro. If you're not entertaining me, what the fuck use are you?"

Levi looked at Albert and gasped just as Lyndon cursed. Although Albert had shorter hair, he looked like Lyndon's carbon copy. How had he missed the resemblance? It was one thing to know Lyndon's stalker was a sibling, but to see how much they looked alike made it almost impossible for Levi to shift and kill the man.

Yet when he swung his head back around and watched Lyndon shift from cougar to man then back again, when he heard Albert's laughter, Levi knew he had no other choice. He could only hope his shift would go unnoticed. He rarely got through it without mewling because it fucking hurt.

There was a snap of a twig, then a subtle change in the direction of the wind. Levi hesitated for a second then panic ramped on top of the fear already clawing at him. *Oscar!* He wasn't dead! No, he was in shifted form, and he was stalking his prey.

Levi saw the pale blue eyes in the foliage. In the instant their gazes caught, he knew without a doubt what his brother was going to do. Before he could think of an alternative or so much as gesture for him to wait, Oscar slunk away. He moved in behind Albert a good six yards. And as much as Levi didn't want to have to kill Lyndon's brother, he didn't want Lyndon killed, either. He was afraid it could happen when Oscar pounced — which he was going to do, because he was stealthily creeping towards Albert. Oscar, low to the ground, silent as a thought, was a deadly, beautiful sight. One Lyndon, his vision blocked by Albert's body, couldn't see. He wouldn't know when to duck.

Which meant it was up to Levi, then. Maybe that was why Oscar had made sure to get his attention.

## Levi

The bare sound of the twig snapping had gone unnoticed by the other two men, but not by Levi.

Levi glanced at Oscar, thought he saw something in his eyes confirming his suspicions, but it could have been his own wishful thinking. Oscar was closer now, almost within distance for a quick, deadly attack.

*I should have shifted.* There was no time for it now. Levi checked Oscar's position, gave a small nod, then he leapt, throwing himself between Lyndon and Albert. The sound of the gunfire caused him to stiffen, his arms tightening around Lyndon as they hit the ground.

Lyndon's gasp was eradicated by the whizz of a bullet shooting past Levi's ear. It was so close his skin felt scorched, but he didn't have a second to think on that before a shrill scream split the air.

"Levi." Lyndon moaned his name, relief and pain making his voice thick. Levi rolled to his other side, not wanting Lyndon to see Oscar's attack on Albert. As soon as he had them rolled, though, Levi saw it, or what was left of the attack. Oscar hadn't played around, making the kill quick. Oscar's white coat was splattered with more blood than the leopard's rosettes and Albert's neck was — Levi closed his eyes and held onto Lyndon.

Lyndon was so still in Levi's arms, didn't try to see what was happening. Those two things combined with the wave of sorrow rolling off Lyndon told Levi his lover knew about or had maybe even seen Oscar's attack. Albert was already dead by the time Lyndon had seen him one last time.

Levi held Lyndon, murmuring comforting words as Lyndon trembled and Oscar shifted. Minutes later, a soft touch on his arm startled Levi into opening his eyes. Oscar knelt behind Lyndon, looking miserable and proud at the same time. His eyes begged for something from Levi, and Levi didn't hesitate to give it to him. Even though it was the last thing he felt like doing, Levi smiled and didn't have to fake it, not when he was so relieved Lyndon and Oscar were alive. But, "Where's Drake and Orion?"

Lyndon shuddered and twisted his head enough that Levi thought he could see Oscar. Oscar blanched and tried to move back but Lyndon showed his quick speed by grabbing Oscar's wrist. "Where are your brothers?"

Oscar gulped and didn't seem to know where to look. "They should be waking up, I hope. They were hit twice by those darts—Drake three times, I think. I just got one, probably because of my size. Drake tried to fight, I guess. He has some gouges, so does Orion but it looks like his is from falling against a big rock." Oscar tried to stand again but Lyndon didn't release his wrist.

Instead Lyndon pulled against Levi's hold on him. Levi let up and watched as Lyndon rolled onto his back then pulled Oscar down, halfway on his chest. Lyndon wrapped Oscar in a hug and said roughly, "It's...it's okay, Oscar. I'm not mad at you. I'm grateful, really. I just wish there'd been another way— but there wasn't," Lyndon added when Oscar sniffled. "There wasn't. Albert was nothing like you or your brothers. He was full of hate and greed. You did something that was hard for you, I know it was, yet you didn't hesitate. You weren't selfish. I'd be honoured if you'd let me call you brother."

Oscar's answer turned into a sob, and Levi reached for his brother and Lyndon, pulling them into an awkward but comforting embrace. He held them as well as he could until his dad and brothers found them.

# Chapter Twenty-Three

Lyndon was grateful Levi's family was willing to hold off on much of the questions they had until the next day. Oscar answered what he could, but he hadn't heard all of the exchange between Lyndon and Albert. When he'd had to explain how all of his father's children were being pitted against each other, he'd thought Marybeth was going to hunt his father down. He'd worried about it enough that he'd pointed out his father's death wouldn't change the will.

Marybeth had answered with an avowal about how the will could be fixed before the man's death.

Lyndon was kind of in awe of the woman, and kind of scared of her. And he still didn't know how they were going to get his father to change his will, or if Marybeth had some diabolical plan in mind she wasn't sharing with him. It wouldn't surprise him if that were the case.

"How are you feeling?" Marybeth asked him, giving him a long look that encompassed his entire body.

"I hurt," Lyndon admitted, seeing no use in even trying to lie. The way Albert had clawed him in the side, almost exactly where his father had, seemed fitting. Wounds from his family, nowhere near as deep as the ones he'd carry inside. His shoulder had needed stitches, and that had been a painful experience Lyndon didn't ever care to repeat. The other gashes and bruises he had would heal soon enough, but in all honesty he was more worried about Oscar, and he knew everyone else was, too.

Looking around the den in Henry and Cheryl's house, he noticed Oscar had slipped away. Despite the warmth of the room, made cosy by clusters of pictures and paintings as well as carvings by Levi, Lyndon felt a chill when he realised Oscar was gone.

"How is he?" he asked Marybeth.

Levi gave him a watery smile and stood up. "I'm going to go check on him."

Marybeth watched Levi leave before answering. "He knows he did what he had to do, but killing takes a toll on one's soul—if they've got a soul."

Guilt ate at Lyndon as it had ever since Oscar had ended Albert's life. "I'm sorry, Marybeth. If I could—"

"No." She cut him off firmly, cutting her hand through the air between them. "None of that. It happened as it had to. Oscar is strong. *So* many people don't see it. They see a cute little boy with a messed-up hand, and they're stupid for being so blind. If you'd have had to kill your half-brother, it would have done more harm to you than it did to Oscar. It's worse when the life you take belongs to someone you should care about but can't because of—" Marybeth shook her head and looked away. "Oscar also worries about what he has done. He's afraid eventually you'll hate him for it. I told him you were a better man than he was giving you credit for being, but you'll have to reassure him."

"I will." Lyndon would tell Oscar every day, as often as he had to until Oscar believed Lyndon didn't hate him for Albert's death. That was all on Albert's soul, and their father's. If they didn't have souls, well, there was a debate Lyndon wasn't up to. But Albert and their father had made their choices, forcing an innocent man to commit an act he should never have had to make. Lyndon had made his choices as well, and doing so meant accepting this family and the place in it they offered him. Taking care of them, and, he was sure, loving Levi. The kernel of the emotion was there, growing stronger each moment they spent together. He knew it was only a matter of time before he had to confess it, before his heart swelled and the need to speak the words couldn't be repressed.

But something had been pricking at his mind ever since Marybeth had said it. He scooted forward on the chair until he was almost knee to knee with Marybeth. She gave him a smile that made him think she knew just what he was going to ask. He was tempted to ask her some off-the-wall question just to throw her, but he figured she'd probably know the damned answer to it.

"You know what I'm wondering," he began, and Marybeth's uptilted lips confirmed it. Lyndon ploughed ahead, sure she wouldn't just tell him unless he asked. "You mentioned knowing something about what was happening between Levi and me, or thinking you might. Have you had a chance to figure it out?"

Marybeth stood and held out her hand to him. "Come outside, get some fresh air. I feel like taking a walk."

*Okay then, a private conversation it is.* Lyndon placed her hand on his forearm and crooked his elbow enough so they were both comfortable then he escorted her outside. Once they were on a well-worn pebbled path sheltered by thick tree limbs overhead, Marybeth began to talk.

"I don't remember a whole lot about my people. Our people. I was only six when my family was killed. But there are little bits of information still floating around here." She tapped her temple. "Sometimes it's hard to tell what was a dream and what was real, which was why I said I needed some time. But, I think I'm remembering right. There were pairs in our clan who were mates." She stopped and turned to face him, her eyes burning into his. "Not just couples who paired up, but mates whose souls called to one another. My parents were like that. I thought it was a false memory for a long time, because what child doesn't want to remember their parents being happy and thoroughly in love? But I saw you and Levi, and I started thinking, and not just about you two, but about all the couples in our family. I remember my father saying mates would find each other no matter the distance, if possible. No one else would satisfy them. Those couples who were together and in love, without the same instinctive drive, I guess they didn't have mates."

She shrugged. "I don't know about for sure. I thought it was only something that happened between snow leopards, but I met Vincent and never once wanted another man. Maybe it isn't as strong an instinct if our mate is human, or maybe we simply call it true love, but what I see between you and Levi reminds me of my parents. They were incredibly happy together."

Lyndon frowned even as his pulse kicked up a few notches. "Why didn't you want to tell me this inside?"

"Because Henry and Cheryl are in love and as devoted to each other as two people can be," she said, looking at him like he just wasn't very bright. "How do you think they would feel if they knew there was such a thing as mates? Granted, I think their love is just as strong, but humans don't have the same instinctual drives we shifters do. I wouldn't want Henry to feel that he was inferior, or worse even, depriving Cheryl of her true mate."

"But—" Lyndon's head was starting to pound, he was frowning so hard. "You said it might just be what people call true love in humans. Don't you think maybe it's the same thing? Maybe the intensity isn't as ramped up at first, but shifters have instincts that help guide us. A human would be more logical, maybe even instinctively fearful of a shifter. It doesn't mean—in my opinion—that humans and shifters don't have mates. You said yourself you never wanted anyone else once you met Vincent, and Levi had told me there were no divorces in the family. Don't you think there's a good chance I'm right?"

Marybeth considered it for a minute, then another, and Lyndon thought she just wasn't going to answer him.

"Maybe," she finally admitted. "I just don't want our non-shifter family members feeling like they're less than the shifter family members. That's why I would prefer to keep this between us, and Levi, of course, at least for now." She took a step back and turned a little then she peered over her shoulder. "And Oscar, I suppose. Levi, you and your brother get out here."

Lyndon couldn't keep back a grin when the brothers stepped out from a thick clump of trees looking like guilty children.

"Sorry Grandma Marybeth," they both muttered.

## Levi

Lyndon lifted one arm and Levi settled in beneath it, pressing carefully against Lyndon's side.

"Come here, you," Levi said to Oscar, then the three of them stood facing Marybeth.

"Now, obviously I knew you two were out there because I am just that sharp." Marybeth looked very pleased with herself about it, too. "Levi needed to know, and you, Oscar." She cupped her grandson's chin. "You and Levi will be our family's story-tellers. You've both always listened and observed, and I know you keep every bit of it in those sharp brains of yours."

Oscar looked poleaxed, his mouth dropping open and his eyes widening. He didn't exactly appear thrilled, in Lyndon's opinion. Not that he was going to speak up as Oscar continued sputtering. "But—but I—" Levi just looked very...intense.

"But nothing," Marybeth scoffed. "My father was the youngest and he was our storyteller. I had a brother, the youngest brother—I think he was three or four years older than me—who was supposed to take over when my father passed." The sadness creeping into her eyes didn't appear to have dulled any during the intervening years since her loss. "He was killed. I've watched you two since you were both born, and my heart tells me this is right. Whether my first clan had one or a dozen storytellers, that doesn't matter. What does matter is these."

She placed a hand over each of the brother's hearts. "Your hearts beat good and strong. The blood of our ancestors pumps through them, filling you both with the desire for knowledge about our people. Timothy, his heart beats with it as well. The three of you will make sure what I know is passed down." She nodded once. "And since Timothy is going back to my homeland to search for more snow leopard shifters, for more knowledge, hopefully the three of you will keep our family united and enduring."

Marybeth patted both men's chests then tipped her head towards the house. "Now, that's enough deep thoughts for the day. I want to be escorted back by three handsome men."

Oscar stepped forward and held out his arm. "Well, I'm sorry there's only one here to escort you."

Lyndon laughed, and Levi chortled too. He thought Marybeth was right. Oscar was going to be okay; he was strong, much stronger than he looked.

As for him and Levi, well, they were going to have a long, happy life together as mates, lovers, and best friends. Everything else, they'd handle as it came.

# Epilogue

One thing Levi couldn't deny, he had a man who wasn't hesitant or timid. Lyndon was spread out on the bed on his back, naked as the day he was born, legs bent at the knees so his heels almost touched his ass cheeks. His arms were spread as well, his hands open palms up, relaxed, and his dick was erect and wet-tipped.

As gorgeous as Lyndon was, the hunger in his eyes was a bigger aphrodisiac than everything else. Still, Levi cocked a hip against the door frame as he stared into his lover's golden eyes. "Are you trying to give me a hint, like maybe you're horny?" It wouldn't hurt to tease the sexy man a little.

Lyndon did something then Levi had never seen him do before. He rolled his eyes until all that was showing was the whites, then he rolled them back down so he could glare at Levi. "No, I'm *trying* to get you to fuck me now that I'm healed."

"Oh," Levi said, his cock filling so quickly he was surprised he didn't hurt himself. He was, however, a tad dizzy, either from the rush of blood down south or just from the idea of finally being able to fuck Lyndon again. Or both.

Levi dragged his gaze down Lyndon's body, the sight of all of his lover's muscled, hairy flesh making him bite his lip to keep from babbling in gratitude. He wanted to just dive right in, to fill Lyndon up and ride him until they both collapsed in a pleasurably exhausted pile, too sated to move for hours. God, he could almost come just from thinking about it while he looked at Lyndon. Then he did a double take when he was studying Lyndon's balls, because beneath them, Lyndon's skin glistened.

Levi sniffed, catching the scent of their favourite lube. He couldn't look away from that spot—well, he didn't until Lyndon spread his legs wider, causing his butt to spread, too. Then he saw Lyndon's greased up little hole and damn near came in his pants.

"Fuck fuck fuck," Levi muttered as he took off his clothes. It would have gone faster, he scolded himself silently, had he taken his stupid boots off first. "Can't think when you're spread out like that, just waiting for me." And he couldn't talk in complete sentences and undress at the same time, either, it seemed.

Lyndon's chuckle as Levi hopped around trying to keep from ass-planting on the floor did not help things any at all. By the time Levi got his boots off, he barely had the patience to kick his jeans down his legs. But no way was he fucking Lyndon the first time with anything between them. Marybeth had pointed out that none of the shifters contracted human diseases, not even a cold. Levi had wondered what they'd end up dying from then, but decided it was too depressing a thought to dwell on.

And now, he and Lyndon had discussed tossing the condoms just this morning after Marybeth's little disclosure. Levi was glad he'd asked her about getting tested, and he wondered if she would be telling the rest of the family. He kind of doubted it. Marybeth kept things to herself for reasons no one else could divine, although maybe she didn't want her shifter kin giving themselves away by going out and fucking indiscriminately without rubbers.

*Something to worry about later!* Levi shut off his brain except for the horny part, which was plotting where to lick Lyndon first. *The curve of his shoulder? Or the divot at the base of his spine? The back of his knee — there're too many choices!*

When Lyndon grasped his cock at the root, Levi had his answer. He crawled onto the bed and gripped Lyndon's chin, and kissed him like the smoking-hot, sexy man he was. Levi licked every bit of Lyndon's mouth he could, drinking down the soft moans they both made. He sucked on Lyndon's lips, the top first then the bottom. Lyndon's breath became louder, harsher. He reached for Levi and Levi moved over him, straddling Lyndon's hips in a wide sprawl, arching his back and lowering his chest to Lyndon's.

Levi kept his weight on his elbows. He rutted and it felt so damn good, the way his cock rubbed alongside Lyndon's. The way Lyndon moaned and undulated beneath him stoked every flame of desire burning in Levi. When Lyndon arched up, thrusting as greedily as Levi was, it nearly drove Levi out of his mind. He nipped Lyndon's chin, then his Adam's apple. Lyndon's low groan passed through his throat, the sound vibrating against Levi's lips.

Lyndon's grip tightened on Levi, his claws sharp and black. The licks of pain spiked Levi's need higher. He lifted his head and peered into Lyndon's eyes. "What do you want? Gentle and—"

Lyndon's growl cut him off. "You know what I want! You've been too careful the past two weeks! Stop holding back."

It was true, Levi had been afraid to scratch Lyndon or bite him, not after he'd been torn up like he had.

"It's different with you," Lyndon told him, cradling Levi's cheek. "It isn't anywhere near the same, you have to believe that."

And Levi did, because the need in Lyndon was so strong it was pounding into him. Instead of answering verbally, he grinned then slid down and bit Lyndon's nipple. The raspy hairs tickled his lips, but the shout the bite drew from Lyndon was priceless. Levi pinched and pulled at the other nipple while he tongued and nibbled the first.

Lyndon grabbed Levi's hair. "Stop, oh God stop before I come all over the place!"

Levi stopped then immediately slid down lower and sucked Lyndon's fat dick into his mouth. Lyndon's shout had to have been heard all the way to Holton. He bucked and clutched at Levi's head, holding him in place. Levi hummed around the cock filling his mouth as he fondled Lyndon's balls. He tugged on the tufts of hair, eliciting more delicious sounds from Lyndon. Levi tongued up Lyndon's length, flicking at the sensitive bundle of nerves on the underside of his crown. What sounded like a whimper slipped from Lyndon's lips. Levi flicked that spot again and got the same sound, which delighted him so much he did it had to repeat the move a few more times.

He dragged his cock against Lyndon's leg, humping, rubbing, a little friction to help ease his own need. Then he dove back down on Lyndon's dick, not stopping until he had Lyndon's pubes poking at his nose. He slid a finger into Lyndon's lubed ass, something he'd done almost every time they'd made love. Lyndon wasn't big on slow and easy, not when it came to being penetrated by Levi's fingers.

Another bob of his head, then Levi pushed a second digit into Lyndon. He swallowed around Lyndon's cock, the tip buried in his throat, and Lyndon went off like a firecracker, shouting and bucking, cum spurting from his dick. The silky constriction of Lyndon's ass around Levi's fingers made it necessary for him to reach down and pinch the base of his own cock before he ended up climaxing as well.

Levi closed his eyes and he kept suckling Lyndon's dick, trying to keep what little control he had left. He massaged the spongy gland in Lyndon's ass once he could move his fingers again. Lyndon's cock stayed hard although he wiggled and pulled at Levi's hair again.

Levi backed off enough to raise his up and let Lyndon's cock slip from his mouth.

"Too much," Lyndon explained, pressing his cock against his stomach.

Levi's lips quirked as he slid his hands under Lyndon's ass. "How about this?" He spread Lyndon's cheeks with his thumb, exposing Lyndon's fluttering hole more. "Pull your legs up for me."

Lyndon's breath stuttered but he hooked his hands around the back of his knees and hitched his legs to his chest. The move opened him further, and tipped his ass up, two bonuses. Levi delved in, lapping at the lubed ring. The cherry flavour was kind of appropriate, he thought, though he wished now they weren't using any lube just yet.

*Next time, I'll taste just him.* Lyndon jerked, his butt clenching. Levi speared his tongue into Lyndon's hole and moaned at making one of his fantasies a reality.

He liked getting fucked, loved it, and he certainly loved it when Lyndon rimmed him—but damn, he'd missed doing this, and doing it with Lyndon was tipping Levi into a euphoric state he hadn't yet been in.

Levi tongue-fucked Lyndon until his jaws ached and Lyndon was a squirming, begging mass of need.

"Please, please, Levi! Please fuck me," Lyndon rasped, holding on to Levi's hair as if he were afraid Levi was going to disappear.

Levi's dick was so hard he was afraid he'd come before he even got the head in Lyndon's ass. Still, he was damn sure going to try. He sat up and swiped his mouth off on the back of one hand then hooked his arms around the tops of Lyndon's thighs. One good tug and he had Lyndon's ass in his lap. Levi didn't hesitate. He lined up his cock and pushed in. Heat enveloped his dick in a velvety smooth grip. Levi couldn't stop the shout any more than he could stop shoving into Lyndon's heavenly vice. Lyndon's cry and the way he tried to rock his hips into Levi's lap was almost Levi's undoing.

"Lyndon—" Levi gave up on talking when pleasure rolled up from his balls, suffusing his nerve endings with the sensation so intense it bordered on painful. He thrust into Lyndon's opening, not stopping until his balls slapped Lyndon's ass. It was maddeningly good—almost perfect, except—

Levi hooked his arms around the backside of Lyndon's knees and hitched them up as he spread his legs. He stretched out on top of Lyndon, his knees wedged beside Lyndon's hips. The change in position gave him more depth, and Levi held still as he looked down at Lyndon.

"Move," Lyndon ordered, which was what Levi had needed to hear.

He didn't start out slow and gentle, knowing by the way Lyndon's claws were digging into his shoulders gentle wasn't what Lyndon wanted. Fast and hard, as deep as he could get, Levi fucked Lyndon, the force of his thrusts shoving Lyndon up the bed. Levi pressed on Lyndon's legs more and grabbed Lyndon's shoulders from underneath. He tried to keep his claws from scratching, but Lyndon's snarl snapped him out of the protective mode he'd fallen into. Lyndon neither wanted nor needed coddling when it came to sex. Neither did Levi.

Claws pricked skin, then dug in deeper. Levi slammed into Lyndon's ass. Lyndon gave as good, leaving a trail of scratches down Levi's chest before reaching between them to fist his cock. Lyndon began pumping his length while curling his other hand around Levi's arm. Levi knew he'd have more scratches there, and it made him ram his cock in harder, faster, Lyndon's curses and claws demanding more.

Levi let go of Lyndon's shoulder. "Put your legs around me." Lyndon did, digging his heels into Levi's ass. He lowered himself enough so he could tip his head and find the sweet spot where Lyndon's neck met shoulder. Levi licked the spot while he buried his hands in Lyndon's hair. Lyndon shuddered beneath him. Each jerk of his hand brought Lyndon's fist in contact with Levi's stomach, not painfully so but forcefully enough to remind him of exactly what was happening down there. Lyndon tightened his legs and pulled his hand out from between them, pressing Levi down. Levi thrust, delighting in the way Lyndon's cock was pinned, knowing he was providing the friction to it and would drive Lyndon out of his mind very soon.

Nuzzling the place he'd picked out, Levi fucked Lyndon harder with each stroke. He felt the beginnings of his orgasm in small but increasing waves of electric sparks flitting up from his dick. A flush raced over his skin, warming him, and a tide of ecstasy began to roll through his body. Levi tried to hold on, wanting to wait until Lyndon came, but the tight sheath around his dick and the taste of Lyndon's skin was too much. He pushed his face against the place he'd licked, then bit at the same time the first jet of cum shot from his dick.

Lyndon's immediate cry just barely preceded the hot, wet spunk that splattered onto Levi's stomach. His dick squeezed tight by Lyndon's constricting inner muscles, Levi's hips stuttered and he whimpered as he came in Lyndon's ass. Lyndon's hand stilled between them and Levi pumped the last bit of cum from his dick. He lifted up on his elbows and tried to see the mark he'd left, but his vision was hazy and his head too heavy to hold up.

"Hand," he managed to mutter before he collapsed on top of Lyndon.

"God, Levi that was…" Lyndon huffed and Levi was hugged so hard he almost had to protest. "I can't even describe it. And when you bit me, oh my fucking hell, it was like—"

Levi snorted. Who knew Lyndon would be a chatty bottom? Levi was so fucked out he couldn't hardly breathe, for shit's sake. Still, he listened while Lyndon went on about how 'unfuckingbelievebly good' their mating had been. Levi might have even glowed with the effusive praise.

## Levi

Later, once Levi's brain cells had decided they weren't totally fried, he sat beside Lyndon, their backs supported by the headboard. They finished off the sandwiches Lyndon had made. Levi was still trying to figure out where Lyndon had found the energy to get up and make the sandwiches.

Lyndon set his plate on the floor then cleared his throat. Levi felt the nervousness coming off the man and wondered what was wrong. "Did I do something wrong after all?"

"No, not at all." Lyndon grinned at him for a few seconds. "You did everything very right, I thought I made just how right abundantly clear. This isn't about sex, it's about what Albert said, about there being more of our siblings out there. Will my father find them, try to pit them against each other since Albert is dead? I just keep thinking about it. I don't have the slightest idea of who they'd be or where they'd be, but it worries me."

Levi had thought of that too, but in truth, he couldn't figure out how to discover if Lyndon had any more brothers or sisters. Lyndon's father hadn't even been named on his birth certificate, and Levi would bet Cole Tavares did the same with any other kids he might have had out of wedlock. It didn't really leave them any clues, or any easy way to look, and asking Lyndon's father was definitely out of the question.

"I suppose all we can do for now at least is wait."

Lyndon nodded. "Yeah, I suppose so"

Levi set his plate down and Lyndon pulled him closer. He didn't think he'd ever get tired of this; cuddling and fucking and making love. There there were all the little things, sharing the bathroom mirror, bickering over who did the dishes. It was as close to perfection as he could have wished for.

Levi closed his eyes and rubbed his cheek on Lyndon's chest. Lyndon purred, a sound Levi didn't hear from him often, which made it all the more special. When Lyndon stopped, Levi cracked open his eyes. "What're you thinking?"

"I'm thinking, this is more, you're more, than I ever thought I'd have. And I wish I had your talent. I'd carve you just like this, curled up to me, looking warm and content, looking like home."

"Oh." Levi blinked, a little stunned by Lyndon's admissions. Then he wanted to smack himself for not responding with something more eloquent than 'Oh.' Levi kissed Lyndon's chest. "I'm sorry. You just, you blew me away, Lyndon, and I don't even know what to say. You're incredible, inside and out, and I sound so lame, but I—" Levi swallowed when he ran out of words. He cleared his throat and murmured, "Just don't leave me, okay? If you feel like you have to roam, take me with you."

God, he sounded like a needy twit, but…he needed Lyndon. He couldn't hide it.

"I have no reason to roam anymore," Lyndon pointed out. "And I've got every reason to stay right here with you." He stroked Levi's back, a sure caress guaranteed to soon lull him into sleep. "Besides, I have a family here to watch over."

"You do," Levi assured him, so happy he thought he'd just burst with it. Then he tipped his head back and waited for Lyndon to meet his gaze. When he did, the warm gold colour seemed to glow, as if lit internally. "Your family loves you, you know. I love you." It came out so easily, and here Levi had been trying to keep it back for fear of—*what? Saying it first? Well, it appears I am an idiot! Especially considering the way Lyndon's smiling at me now! Shoulda told him as soon as I realised it.*

Lyndon rolled Levi onto his back, covering Levi with his strong, muscled body. He framed Levi's face in his hands, sinking his fingers into Levi's hair. "I love you too."

Levi smiled and nuzzled against Lyndon's palm. "Good." And it was. After spending a week with his cousins, listening to them going on about their love lives, Levi had been left feeling like he'd never have anyone. But now he had this incredible man to spend his life with. Levi opened for him, offering Lyndon everything, and he knew whatever happened in the future, they could handle it, as long as they had each other.

# About the Author

A native Texan, Bailey spends her days spinning stories around in her head, which has contributed to more than one incident of tripping over her own feet. Evenings are reserved for pounding away at the keyboard, as are early morning hours. Sleep? Doesn't happen much. Writing is too much fun, and there are too many characters bouncing about, tapping on Bailey's brain demanding to be let out.

Caffeine and chocolate are permanent fixtures in Bailey's office and are never far from hand at any given time. Removing either of those necessities from Bailey's presence can result in what is know as A Very, Very Scary Bailey and is not advised under any circumstances.

Bailey Bradford loves to hear from readers. You can find her contact information, website details and author profile page at http://www.total-e-bound.com.

# Total-E-Bound Publishing

www.total-e-bound.com

Take a look at our exciting range of literagasmic™ erotic romance titles and discover pure quality at Total-E-Bound.

Made in the USA
Lexington, KY
23 August 2013